BARNUM'S ANGEL

THE PALE CHRONICLES
BOOK ONE

LEN BOSWELL

Black Rose Writing | Texas

ISBN: 978-1-68513-038-1
PUBLISHED BY BLACK ROSE WRITING
www.blackrosewriting.com

Printed in the United States of America
Suggested Retail Price (SRP) $20.95

Barnum's Angel is printed in Book Antiqua

*As a planet-friendly publisher, Black Rose Writing does its best to eliminate unnecessary waste to reduce paper usage and energy costs, while never compromising the reading experience. As a result, the final word count vs. page count may not meet common expectations.

PRAISE FOR
BARNUM'S ANGEL

"A masterwork, with likable characters, a captivating plot, and an absolutely original blend of reality and fantasy. "
—The Historical Fiction Company, *Book of the Year Awards*

"Everything readers want from great literature . . . A tour de force of tension, humor, perspective, and spectacle."
—Michael Hartnett, *The Blue Rat*

"Magical. Historical fantasy at its best!"
—Courtney Filigenzi, *Clover Doves*

"Astonishing!"
—Net Galley Review

AWARDS

GOLD AWARD for 2023 Best Historical Fantasy
—The Historical Fiction Company, *Book of the Year Awards*

5-Star Highly Recommended Award
—The Historical Fiction Company

Finalist Award, American Fiction Awards

To all I love without condition
To all I love without omission

Never Doubt

BARNUM'S ANGEL

"I am not very proud of being a human being; in fact, I distinctly dislike the species in many ways. I can readily conceive of beings vastly superior in every respect.
—H. P. Lovecraft

"No naturalist has devoted more painstaking attention to the structure of the barnacles than Mr. Darwin."
—Richard Owen

"As a general thing, I have not 'duped the world' nor attempted to do so... I have generally given people the worth of their money twice told."
—P. T. Barnum

"Often a cold shudder has run through me, and I have asked myself whether I may have not devoted myself to a fantasy."
—Charles Darwin

PROLOGUE

Aboard HMS *Beagle*, Port Famine, Strait of Magellan, Tierra del Fuego, August 2, 1828.

When you go to sea, you take five things along: you, your mates, your ship, the sea, and the weather, and any one of those could be your ruin.

Georgie had to shake his head every time he thought of those words, the cheery final words of advice his father had given him many months ago as they stood on the docks saying their farewells. Georgie had shrugged them off—his father was famous for saying just the wrong thing at just the wrong time—but today the words seemed most apt, at least concerning the weather.

George "Little Georgie" Derbishire, the youngest midshipman aboard, had learned too well that the sea and the weather should never be trusted, but he had faith in his mates and his ship, and after more than two years at sea, had faith in himself, the weak, skinny boy who'd set sail transformed into a robust lad broad of chest and two hands taller, his arms and legs knotted with muscle. By rights, he should have been called "Big George" or even "King George," but the original moniker handed down by the crew had stuck to him as much as his cold, salt-encrusted trousers stuck to him now.

The weather was definitely having its say about things. He was cold to the bone, his breath white as steam from a kettle as he struggled to rise from his hammock in the midshipmen's berth. His father, safely in his cozy parlor back in England, no doubt enjoying an after dinner smoke and railing at Georgie's mum about the slow progress on the building of London Bridge, would have referred to this morning's weather as an annoying but harmless pea-souper. Georgie's mate Chaffer, on the other hand, an overly talkative seaman accused by many of being a word spigot, a man with enough tongue for two sets of teeth, would have reached back into his never-ending store of sea lore and proclaimed today "a day for demons," a day of foreboding.

But Chaffer wasn't proclaiming anything right about now. He was fast asleep, sawing lumber in his hammock at the same time that poor Georgie was scrambling to tug on his shoes and take his post on deck. Not that Chaffer wouldn't have been right about the demons.

Indeed, the morning had begun in a way to provoke even the most docile demons. A cold overnight rain had given way to a thick icy fog, turning the men on deck into ghostly ciphers, all sounds magnified and strangely distorted, the ship's bell endlessly echoing the change of watch in the eerie, still dim light.

Georgie took one step onto the deck, and froze.

One seaman said what made them stop in their tracks was a shrill, terrifying shriek, but others thought the sound was more like the kind of creaking that came from the twisted lines of a ship at anchor as it pitched and rolled in the cold swirling waters. All agreed the next sound was a gunshot, a sharp report coming from the captain's cabin. But Cooper, a seaman said to have such keen hearing that he could detect the lapping of waves on land from twenty kilometers at sea, said that he heard something more within the echoes that followed: the flapping of giant wings, as if some unholy angel had come for the soul of the captain.

In the days that followed, everyone would have an opinion about what had happened, and why, none quite as fantastical as Cooper's, but much embellished nonetheless, stories they were more than eager to share throughout the rest of the voyage: at meals, on deck, after their rum, or high above in the rigging. He was melancholy, he was insane, he was incompetent, he was superstitious, he saw things no one else saw, or he was a right Jonah, bad luck, and they were well rid of him.

One thing was clear: Commander Pringle Stokes, first captain of HMS Beagle, had turned a pistol on himself.

Charles "Puddin'" Davis, his cook, said he had seen this coming for many weeks. "The captain ate less and less, even refused my pudding, and everyone loves my pudding, so no, I am not surprised at all."

Arthur "Muley" Mellersh, a young seamen of legendary stubbornness, whatever the task at hand, said he should have known. "He was just not right. Would stare at the horizon, he would, all funny like, as if he were expecting the devil his self to rise from the sea."

Peter "Windy" Chaffers, that tongue among men, was uncharacteristically succinct: "This place here is the arsehole of the world and shites out even the best of men."

Benjamin "Benny Blood" Bynoe, the assistant surgeon, who helped in the aftermath, when gangrene set in and his patient began rambling on and on about monsters, was the most philosophical. "He was a good man, a good captain in his way, but clearly troubled and out of his head at the end. Everyone has an opinion, some wild and fantastical, but I doubt we will ever know what really prompted him to do this. We all have our demons, do we not?"

Commander Stokes had his demons, all right, and thanks to his uncle, was no stranger to suicide, the "always cheerful" man having taken his life years ago as surcease from the unbearable travails of life. Not that Stokes hadn't suffered travails of his own. The seemingly unending cold and gloom of Tierra del Fuego alone was sufficient to mark a man like Stokes for despair and death. And if that weren't enough, his bungling of the coastal surveys would surely end his career. So why go on, why suffer the dishonor, let alone the wrath of the admiral? Why not join his uncle in blessed oblivion?

If there were a hundred reasons for ending it all, Commander Pringle Stokes was ignoring all but one that morning: fear. Every sound, every smell, every movement of the ship, every candle-blowing puff of wind swirling through the cramped cabin was reason for alarm.

He had locked himself in his cabin four weeks earlier, and with the exception of ever angrier replies to the cook's persistent pleas that he eat more, had not said more than a few words to anyone, save for routine instructions shouted, or more often whispered, through the door to Lieutenant Skyring, his assistant surveyor, who had all but taken complete command of the ship. Not even a visit by a delegation of the native Fuegians that morning could budge him to even open the door a crack. He knew what the miserable savages would say. Appease the beast, do its bidding, take this very god with you, and end our days of fear and terror. Not in such fine words, mind, but in the discordant grunts and wild gestures common to these filthy natives.

He glanced at the little pistol on the table. He had only to cock it, raise it to his temple, and pull the trigger. That quick, that easy, but he still held out some hope that the beast would change its mind and let him and the *Beagle* sail away to England without it. Two weeks had passed, after all.

No, the beast would come, and there would be nowhere to hide. There would only be this simple choice: a quick shot to the head or a fatal confrontation with a beast that could violently rip him apart with its fangs and talons.

He had seen just such a display only weeks earlier, when he had first encountered the beast on Mount Tarn. It had come out of nowhere, swooping down from the sky to attack a guanaco he was hunting and tearing it apart in seconds, greedily consuming its flesh, hide and all. He could not forget the look in the beast's eyes as it leveled its fierce gaze on him, blood dripping from its fangs. Then, even more terrifying, it had spoken to him, in *English!*

He shuddered and picked up the pistol, his hand trembling. The gun seemed to grow heavier every day, and despite the relative warmth of the cabin, it remained cold to the touch. He set it back down, clasped both hands together to stop the shaking, and looked at the door. He knew he had only to open it, invite in his lieutenants, and explain the situation.

He attempted a wry laugh, but it came out as a nervous, almost unhinged, cackle. No, they would think him even madder than they already did for locking himself in his cabin. How does a captain of a British naval vessel explain his belief in a primitive culture's god, a mythical beast now made terrifyingly manifest? A beast that *speaks!*

He jumped from his chair, startled by a sound at the door, a slow, steady scraping sound, as if a single talon were being drawn down the door toward its latch. He reached for the pistol.

PART ONE

Whenever I think of Mr. Barnum, and I must tell you, I think of him less and less as the years pass, I invariably think of that morning when the wagon's doors were flung open by Mr. Partly, may the Devil take his soul, and I saw this tall, imposing man in a top hat, his eyes growing wide as he took me in, his smile growing as he realized I was what he would later call me: "A first-rate attraction!"

I can't remember his features all that well — time has a way of softening and blurring our memories — but given my heightened sense of smell, I can tell you that he smelled of violet water, liberally applied, a smell I quickly came to loathe.

— Lily, *Interview with the Dragon* (excerpt)

1

Barnum Residence, Grafton Street, West End, London, June 5, 1844.

He checked his watch again and looked out onto the street. The man was late, by a good twenty minutes, which annoyed Phineas Barnum no end. The gall of the man to be late, when all Phineas wanted to do was help him. Yes, he might help himself in the bargain—it would only be fair after all—but his interest was to see if this act would make a good attraction, both here and in America. If it could, he'd pay the man a handsome sum. If it could not, the man would at least have a better act.

He glanced in the mirror near the door, what he called *the last chance to look his best* before he ventured into the world, which more and more seemed his for the taking. His wide-set blue eyes stared back at him, and he couldn't help but smile and wink at the self-proclaimed "Prince of Humbugs" who stared back. His nose may have been a tad bulbous, but he was still a handsome man, as he had said to himself and others on many occasions. He ran a hand through his dark curly hair, which had already receded quite far for a young man of 34 years. His royal blue tie was out of place, too. He straightened it around the standing collar of his white linen shirt, which was too damnable tight, and tucked it off to the left under his black, double-breasted vest, as was the fashion.

Then he stood back a bit from the mirror to get a good view of his black frock coat, brushing at the dandruff on his shoulders. He was an inch or two above six feet tall and thought himself a fine figure of a man, vest-controlled paunch notwithstanding. Finally satisfied, he turned away from the mirror, walked back to the window, and pulled his gold watch from his vest pocket once more. *Damnable man!*

And then he heard the sound of a wagon rolling slowly down the street. It was him at last, Tom Partly, owner-proprietor of a struggling penny show. Barnum grabbed his top hat, placed it on his head at a rakish angle, and walked into the summer morning.

As luxurious as the West End was, the ever present smell of sewage, garbage, and burning coal greeted every nose, however poor or wealthy. The advantage the wealthy had here was the wind, which carried the black soot and putrescent odors—and all the diseases that went with it—into the poor neighborhoods to the east. *Money can even buy you better air*, he thought. He would have to remember that when he returned to New York. *Perhaps a home in Connecticut?*

The wagon came to a stop and Mr. Partly jumped down. The name seemed apt for a man so slight and short, particularly as he stood there next to Barnum, who towered over him. He was dressed, as Barnum had instructed him, in his finest clothes, but looked more like a beggar in costume than an upstanding gentleman, as Barnum had hoped. Even in these fine clothes, the man smelled of sweat and urine.

"Good tidings, Mr. Barnum, and my sincere apologies for my tardiness. Your instructions took longer than I expected."

Barnum had met Partly and his "act" just three days before at a fair in Greenwich, where for a penny each you could see acts like strong men, white Negroes, bearded women, and the like.

In short, nothing that Barnum had not seen a hundred times over in freak shows on both continents. There were even cleverly and not-so-cleverly put together abominations and faux creations like pig boys and squirrel men. It brought to mind one of Barnum's own recent creations, the Fiji Mermaid, a great work of taxidermy involving the head of a monkey and the skeletal tail of a large fish.

The one act that had stood out from all the others was Mr. Partly's "dragon child," not because people were paying to see it in great numbers, the silver lining of any crowd, but that people were running away from the act, clearly disturbed by it, even before money changed hands. That had piqued Barnum's interest. If he could turn that headlong fear into apprehensive fascination, he would have a winner as valuable as his diminutive cousin, Charles Stratton, renamed General Tom Thumb just months ago, now fast asleep upstairs, exhausted by another lucrative command performance.

He gave Partly a smirk. "Well, then, let's have a look."

"Of course." He went to the back of the wagon and swung its doors wide open. The stench was overwhelming.

"I told you to bathe the child!"

"It did not have a mind to bathe, sir. It was all we could do just to follow your instructions."

"If the creature is to be an angel, it must smell like an angel."

"Sir, it do not act like no angel. We did our best."

"All right, then, bring your angel into the light, so I can see your work."

Partly tugged on a thick chain and the creature stepped forward into the light. Barnum gasped.

"Oh, my, this is better than I had hoped, but do we really need the chains?"

"Oh, my, yes, sir."

The girl was tall for a ten-year-old, with skin as white as white can be and long flowing hair that sparkled pale in the morning light. Her eyes seemed purplish red like any other albino, and she had a sweet face, angelic to Barnum's eye. With a somewhat exotic look, almost Polynesian. Maybe a hint of Chinese around the eyes. The floor-length white gown he had provided was a perfect fit.

"Do her hair be right, sir? When I shows her, I hide that white hair under a black wig. Makes her menacing like."

"Oh, god no," said Barnum. "What do you not understand about the concept of an angel? Her hair *must* be white."

Partly shrugged. "Just a thought, sir. It be your show — if we can come to some agreement."

Barnum ignored him and moved on. "Does she understand English, sir?"

"She does. Even reads all the latest books. Taught her by my other albino, Enku, whom I calls Walla-Walla, the White Witch of Wongo-Bongo."

Barnum ignored the comment. He'd seen more than his share of albinos, with just as ridiculous names. "Good," he said.

He directed his attention to the girl. "Young lady, what is your name?"

Partly did not give her a chance to speak. "We calls her Lily, after the white flower."

Barnum ignored him. "Lily, then, have you practiced your performance with your master?"

The girl's voice was raspy, whispery soft. "Yes."

"Speak up, girl, did you say yes?"

"Yes," she hissed loudly, her eyes widening, focused on Barnum, who took a step back.

"There, there, no reason to get upset. We're all friends here."

She tilted her head to one side. "Are we?"

"Indeed, we are," said Barnum, hoping that a firm positive statement would reassure the girl. He decided it had and pressed on.

"As you know, you are to make a series of moves as your master introduces you. Do you know the key words?"

She nodded.

"All right, assume the first position."

The girl closed her eyes and dipped her head down toward her chest, hands clasped prayerfully in front of her.

"Excellent," said Barnum, "an angel in repose. Now, sir, begin your introduction, and remember to give it all the drama you can muster. Drama stirs the pot and brings the crowd to a simmer."

Partly cleared his throat and began, a bit hesitantly at first, but very forceful and dramatic as he got into the spirit of the speech Barnum had written for him.

"Ladies and gentlemen," he began. "I have combed the four corners of the Earth for an attraction worthy of your dear coin."

He raised both arms above his head and looked at the sky.

"But it was not until I looked to the heavens above that I found what you are about to see."

He stopped and turned to Barnum. "At this point, the curtain opens, right?"

"Yes," said Barnum, "and be sure to do it slowly to get the full attention of the crowd. They will see a very angel, and we want that image to sink in." He turned to the girl. "Are you ready, miss?"

She gave a quick nod and rested her chin on her chest again.

"Okay, the curtain opens to reveal you. The crowd is totally fascinated by you." He turned back to the man. "Continue with the introduction, sir."

Partly nodded, cleared his throat again, and continued. "Behold, then, a very angel from Heaven itself, come to Earth to delight and amaze."

The girl slowly unfurled her wings. Barnum smiled. Partly had done a great job transforming her bat-like wings into the wings of an angel. The white feathers had done the trick.

"And now," said Barnum, "we give the audience about ten seconds, no more, to drink in all her angelic qualities."

He counted to ten. "Okay, sir, continue."

"But why, ladies and gentlemen, why is she here with us now on Earth? Has she no heavenly duties? Could it be that she is a *fallen* angel, out of grace with our Lord?"

The girl raised her head and opened her eyes, then her long scaly white tail slowly emerged from under her gown and began writhing like a snake. *Wonderful*, Barnum thought, *just wonderful!*

Partly shouted. "Or is she an angel from *hell itself?!*"

The girl shrieked, her face transforming, mouth elongating, forming a snout with razor sharp teeth, her feet now talons, her forehead covered with strange bumps, scales forming on her neck, her entire aspect frightening to the extreme. If this had been the first time he had seen her transform, he would have been frozen in place, mouth agape, piss rolling down his leg, but only a brief shudder came over him this time before the showman in him regained control.

"And curtain!" shouted Barnum, clapping his hands loudly and turning to Partly. "I cannot emphasize how important it will be to close the curtain quickly. The crowd will not believe what they have just seen. As frightened as they may have been, they will tell their friends, and many will come back for more, paying again and again."

Partly nodded vigorously. "Was it acceptable, then? Did she do it right?"

"Better than right, sir, she was *perfect*." He thought he caught the merest suggestion of a smile on her face.

2

Port Famine, Strait of Magellan, February 2, 1834.

Robert FitzRoy, second captain of the HMS *Beagle*, lowered his knife and fork and stared at the young man across the table from him, who seemed to be dissecting the fish in front of him rather than eating it.

Now in the third year of their voyage, FitzRoy had grown accustomed to such behavior. In truth, he had grown quite fond of this man whose piercing blue-gray eyes could quite dominate anyone in a debate. FitzRoy, an ardent devotee of the suspect science of phrenology — or *bumpology* as he called it — found him to be extremely bright and thoughtful, despite the fact that the young man's thick and hooded beetle brows and flattened nose suggested quite the opposite. He was a tall man, just under six feet, but with a stoop that made him appear shorter. Thin and wiry at about ten stone, he had dark brown hair that had thinned and receded noticeably since the beginning of the voyage. Robust by any measure, save for off-and-on bouts of sea sickness, he was just days away from turning twenty-five. His clothing varied little from day to day: a dark brown frock coat, blue or brown vest, matching cravat, light brown trousers, and scuffed brown boots. Occasionally, but not today, a shooting jacket and broad-brimmed straw hat.

FitzRoy could bear it no longer. "Oh, Philos, must you dissect everything?"

Charles Darwin, the ship's "natural philosopher," affectionately known as *Philos* by the crew, glanced up briefly before continuing his dissection. "Will you please remind Davis, Fuller, and the rest of the crew to notify me when they've caught something? I have never seen the like of this one—just look at that dorsal fin. And the cooking has quite spoiled its coloration."

FitzRoy rolled his eyes. "Darwin, we must have had this very fish two score times over the past year. I can identify it by its smell alone."

Darwin shook his head. "*Like* this fish, but not *this* fish. What we have here," he said, pointing to the fin with his knife, "is an adaptation, for what or why I can't say, but clearly like no other fish that has been placed in front of me." He rapped his knuckles on the table for emphasis.

FitzRoy abruptly put down his knife and fork, wiped his mouth, and pushed back in his chair. "You have quite spoiled my appetite. I think from now on we will just serve some of that dreadful meat from Kilner and Moorsom, or perhaps just biscuits and the weevils of the day."

He paused, noting that Darwin was not reacting to his attempt at humor. "But very well, I will remind the crew—*again*—that any and all fish must pass your hallowed eyes before they are gutted and cooked."

Darwin nodded, pleased. "Thank you, sir."

FitzRoy sucked at his teeth, a habit Darwin had grown used to over the voyage. "Now, what is so important that cannot wait till morning? It has been a long day, what with this miserable weather and this late meal, and I would sooner to bed."

They had pulled into the cold harbor in a driving rain, and from the look of it, the rain would continue for days, icing the halyards and soaking anything and anyone on the deck of this small ship, barely 90 feet long and 24 feet wide, the cramped, damp home for more than 70 souls, and leaving patches of snow on Mount Tarn, which loomed over the harbor some 2600 feet above the sea.

The HMS *Beagle* had been commissioned for a second voyage on July 4, 1831, and after refitting and provisioning at the Devonport docks, had set sail on 27 December for South America. It was the beginning of the second year of the reign of William IV. Earl Grey was prime minister, with the Whigs in full control. The long wait for London Bridge to open was over, and the English translation of a new novel by Victor Hugo, *The Hunchback of Notre Dame*, was selling briskly in the shops and stalls of London.

Their survey mission was going well. In the past three years they had seen and surveyed the Cape Verde Islands and the eastern coast of South America, with stops in Rio de Janeiro and Montevideo, among others, as well as the Falklands and parts of the Straits of Magellan.

They had also completed their secondary mission: repatriating three young Fuegians that FitzRoy had abducted on the previous voyage. FitzRoy had taken them hostage in an attempt to pressure the Fuegians to return a stolen whaleboat, but when that had failed, he had decided to take them to England, teach them English and civilized ways, and return them, along with a young English missionary, so that they might teach other Fuegians English and the ways of the empire.

In a few more weeks, when they arrived back in Woolya, the site of the new settlement, they would have a chance to see how well that mission was going. FitzRoy was extremely anxious about what they might find. Would the three young Fuegians — York Minster, Jemmy Button, and Fuegia Basket — even be there, or would they have shed their English clothes, slathered their bodies with seal oil and blubber, and disappeared into the wilderness? Had the young missionary, Richard Matthews, still a teenager, been able to prevent the theft-prone Fuegians from stealing everything in sight? FitzRoy had experienced their unceasing demands on the first voyage, their imploring cries of "yammerschooner, yammerschooner" (give me, give me) ringing in his ears.

Darwin could tell FitzRoy had dropped into deep thought, as was his custom—most of their meals were typically spent in silence—and he wasn't sure whether to press the matter or let it drop for the night. He was tired as well, but he could not shake what the ship's carpenter, May, had told him that morning.

"Tell me about the death of Pringle Stokes."

FitzRoy blanched and looked away.

3

Outside the Barnum Residence, Grafton Street, West End, London, June 5, 1844.

Partly waited for Mr. Barnum to make his way back to his residence and close the door behind him before he turned back to Lily.

"Now, then, off with the costume, me dear," he said, reaching out for her. "Can't be soilin' it further."

Lily backed away, forcing him to climb into the back of the wagon. He tapped his ever-present cudgel on his palm as warning. "Now, now, we wants our chicken, does we not? But not in a white dress, does we?"

The promise of food was enough. Lily quickly began to undress, Partly assisting her with the chains, one by one, then reattaching them.

"Take care with those feathers. Careful but quick, see."

Lily complied, finally handing him the dress and the artificial wings, her own wings now folded and tucked within her back. She could tell he was looking at her nakedness, what Enku called her "privatest parts."

"You grows more beautiful each day, me dear," he said, leering at her. "Not long now." He let out an appreciative cluck, then tucked the costume under his arm, jumped down from the wagon, and went to the front, returning seconds later with a small cage containing a chicken.

"Here now, best take it and sit. Time to go." He handed her the cage and slammed the doors shut, leaving her in semi-darkness, the only light slanting in from cracks in the planks that formed the walls and ceiling to the wagon. She could hear him fix the latch and walk to the front of the wagon, which soon began to move down the street, the sound of the wheels on the cobbles growing more rapid by the second.

She felt for the latch to the cage, the chicken nervously ruffling its feathers as she reached in and grabbed it by the neck. It was gone in five bites.

4

Barnum Residence, Grafton Street, West End, London, June 5, 1844.

Barnum burst into the house, slamming the door behind him and tossing his hat on the nearest table.

"Tom," he shouted up the staircase, "come quick!"

General Tom Thumb, real name Charles Stratton, appeared at the top of the stairs and began his slow march down, already dressed in his Napoleon costume, complete with bicorn hat, blue waistcoat with gold-fringed epaulets, red trousers, white belt with miniature sword and scabbard, and tall black boots that had the effect of making him seem even shorter than his proclaimed height of just under two feet. He was just seven years old, but Barnum passed him off as thirteen to emphasize that the General was not about to grow even an inch.

"Why are you dressed so soon?" said Barnum.

The General's voice, through practice, could command a room, and had an air of nobility even in casual conversation. "Practice, sir," he intoned, "practice."

Barnum got right to the point. "So what did you think?"

"Think, sir? Of what?"

"Do not play games, Tom. I saw you at the window."

The General marched by Barnum and into the drawing room, where he climbed on a tufted red-velvet chair, Barnum following him in and sitting opposite him. "All I could see was the man, and I took him to be a ruffian in lord's clothes."

Barnum nodded. "You are right about that, sir. I will have to clean him up a bit, buy him new clothes."

"Perhaps that will work, but his voice sounded shrill, at least from my vantage point at the bedroom window."

"I will work with him, just as I worked with you. Now, what did you think of the girl?"

The General shook his head. "Nothing. The wagon blocked my view. All I could see was the tips of white wings."

"Those were not *her* wings, of course, but she does *have* wings. She is a bona fide attraction, just like you. And she is beautiful in the bargain, and just ten. An albino, certainly, but more than that. She looks to be from the Orient, but not purely so. Her nature is mixed, I am sure. And she has wings, *real* wings, and teeth, sharp teeth."

The General frowned back at him. "She sounds more beast than human. Can she speak?"

"She can, but this act does not require her to say a single word."

"Act?" said the General, looking worried.

Barnum caught the look. "Now, Tom, there is no need for jealousy. You will still be the main attraction, wherever we perform."

The General puffed out a sigh of relief. "And how do you plan to draw a crowd to see her?"

"Why, with *your* crowds, sir. You should know by now that nothing draws a crowd like a crowd. We'll start tonight, in Piccadilly, at the baroness Rothschild's mansion."

"You will bring the girl there?"

"No, of course not. You will be the one and only attraction, but I will talk up the new act. Then we need only engage a theatre, again with you as the featured attraction."

"But when will we meet the queen? You promised me."

Barnum sighed. He had heard this same appeal every day since their arrival. "In due course, Tom. I will have a word with the baroness."

"And would you show this girl to the queen as well?"

Barnum thought back on the girl's transformation from angel to beast. "No, Tom, I think not."

5

Port Famine, Strait of Magellan, February 2, 1834.

FitzRoy pushed back in his chair and stood, placing both hands on the table and leaning across it to loom over Darwin. He was a man of slight build, with a narrow, almond-shaped face made remarkable by a thin, aquiline nose and a wisp of a moustache seemingly brushed in over thin, almost feminine lips. His hair was dark brown and matted down from humidity and the hours he had spent today in his bicorn hat. He had doffed the hat and taken off his rain cape and "undress" uniform coat before the meal, and now stood before Darwin in his white vest and trousers. The overall effect was an aspect of competence, even arrogance, an aristocratic look he used to great effect as a leader of men. A man of quick, sometimes uncontrollable temper, he could by posture and gesture alone impose his will on anyone.

"I don't know what you have heard, sir, or from whom, but the answer to your question is quite simple. Mr. Stokes was a fine officer but given to melancholy and dark moods, as many men are in these gloomy waters. He shot himself in the head, in this very port, some years ago, lingering for many days before his unfortunate death."

Darwin would not be loomed over. He stood so the two of them could talk as equals. "I do not doubt those facts, sir, but let me tell you what I have heard, so that you might comment."

FitzRoy nodded. "Go on, then."

Darwin motioned him to his seat. "Might we sit, sir, this could take a few minutes, and I know you are tired."

"As you wish."

They both sat down, FitzRoy sighing and leaning back in his chair, arms crossed, clearly annoyed and defensive. "Well, then, get on with it."

Darwin cleared his throat. "I was sick earlier this evening and hovering near the rail, gazing out over the harbor, when Mr. May came by to check on me. We talked about the rain and the gloom, and he just came out with this fantastical story about the death of Mr. Stokes."

FitzRoy snorted and shook his head. "Well, of course it was May. He is a fine carpenter, the best in fact, but like so many seamen, is given to superstition and fantasy. Ask him if he believes in mermaids. He does."

Darwin continued. "He recounted a story told to him by a Mr. Cooper, a fellow seaman not among our current crew."

FitzRoy again interrupted. "And for good reason. His drunkenness was legend."

Darwin drummed his fingers on the table. "Might I continue?"

Fitzroy waved his hand dismissively, nodding.

"Cooper, whom I understand was also legendary for his acute hearing, is said to have heard the beating of wings—large wings—just before the shot was fired."

"A billowing sail, the wind, nothing more."

"And yet this Cooper claimed to have *seen* something as well."

"Yes, yes, a strange beast, part dragon, part man, and pale as a sail. This is an old story, cobbled together from hearsay about the ravings of a poor man with a bullet in his brain, talking out of his head and hallucinating."

Darwin paused, wondering whether to continue. "May mentioned that, but said that other seamen on that voyage had reported much the same thing, long before Stokes began his ravings."

"Blather and nonsense."

Darwin shook his head. "I would conclude the same thing had it not been for Jemmy Button, your Fuegian ward."

"Jemmy? What in God's name would Jemmy have to offer on this subject? He was not even there."

"Admittedly, but May said he had made a point of asking Jemmy about this dragon-man early in our voyage, to see if there was any knowledge among the Fuegians of such a creature. And apparently there is. Jemmy knew the word *dragon* and knew where the creature was frequently sighted—right here in Port Famine, atop Mount Tarn."

"That, sir, is impossible. May must be mistaken; Jemmy would not even understand the word, or if he did, he picked it up during his days in England."

"Perhaps, but there is more. He referred to the creature not in English, as a dragon, but in Fuegian, as *the pale man of the mountain*. I suspect other Fuegians may use the same phrase, and—"

FitzRoy exploded. "I am astounded that a man who calls himself a *naturalist*, a *philosopher*, would give the slightest credence to such a fabrication."

Darwin shook his head. "I do not believe for a minute that anyone has seen a dragon or a dragon-man or a man-dragon, but they could have seen a large bird of some kind, as yet unclassified. I am not asking you to believe the story. What I am asking for is a day or so to explore Mount Tarn to see if there is such an avian species. It would be a tremendous scientific find."

FitzRoy sighed, shook his head, and then reluctantly nodded. The *Beagle* would be at harbor for several days, so there would be no harm in granting his request. "It will be a waste of time, but go ahead. We will be here several days before continuing our survey. Take Rowlett and Martens along. If nothing else, perhaps you can return with some guanaco meat, which is much preferable to weevils."

Darwin found the meat of this little relative of the camel to be a bit tough and gamey, but far superior to anything else they had eaten in weeks. Shooting one of these 200-pound sprinters was another matter. They could reach speeds of up to 35 miles per hour, on even the most demanding mountain terrain, a challenging shot for even the likes of Darwin, an expert marksman and experienced hunter.

"Thank you, sir." Darwin rose to leave. "Guanaco it is."

"And Darwin, one other thing."

"Sir?"

"If you come back without evidence of this fantastical creature, you will not mention the subject again in my presence or in any way posit such nonsense to the crew."

6

Rothschild Mansion, Piccadilly, London, Evening of June 5, 1844.

The carriage ride to the Baroness Rothschild's mansion in Piccadilly was uneventful, other than the constant jostling as the wheels raced over the cobbles. The General busied himself repeating long-memorized lines, and Barnum plotted quietly as he watched London pass by through the windows of the carriage.

The carriage soon passed through an imposing gate in a high wall that surrounded a mansion that Barnum would later describe with one word: *noble*. A half-dozen servants, each dressed alike, and quite elegantly, surrounded the coach. They wore black pantaloons and matching coats, with white cravats and vests. White kid gloves completed their outfits. If he had not known they were servants, Barnum would have taken them for the finest gentlemen.

Once inside, an old chap in livery, white wig and all, escorted Barnum and the General up a vast marble staircase and announced their names at the door to the drawing room. The General gasped, as did Barnum, when they entered the room, which was a testament to money and splendor. Couches covered in fine silk damask, elegantly carved gilt chairs, an ebony table with pearl inlays, and mantelpieces chockablock with vases and urns and all manner of things in gold, silver, alabaster, and pearl—even diamonds! And all this lit from above by immense chandeliers.

The baroness herself and the twenty or so guests were all dressed to fit the room. One guest stood out, though, a man of dark copper complexion, an African surely, dressed as his culture dictated: a large loose robe of thick cotton cloth draped in folds around his body; a waistcloth encircling his loins; and wide trousers that ended just above his knees. A small sword hung menacingly at his side.

To Barnum's eye, he would make a worthy attraction, and Barnum wondered whether the man had been brought to the mansion for this very purpose. But such was not the case.

The baroness was quick to introduce all the lords and ladies in attendance, and finally came to the African.

"If it please you, Mr. Barnum, may I introduce the royal envoy from Abyssinia, Biniam Sahle, the son of Emperor Sahle Dengel."

Up close, the man seemed even more a worthy attraction, from his small eyes and flat nose to his close-cropped beard. His large head was topped with what looked like hundreds of carefully coiled ringlets of hair, all greased to a shine and smelling of rancid butter. Most startling of all were his eyebrows, which were totally missing, replaced by a deep cut dyed blue above each eye. It gave him a comical appearance, but Barnum could tell he was a serious man.

"Delighted to meet you, I'm sure," said Barnum.

The man nodded. "It is an honor, sir." He seemed newly practiced in the art of civil conversation.

"Well, then," said the Baroness, "shall we proceed with the entertainment?"

"Indeed, baroness." He gave the General his cue, and the diminutive boy in uniform launched into his practiced performance of songs and imitations, including his signature comical take on Napoleon himself.

As the performance proceeded, the Abyssinian approached Barnum. "I do not understand your people's fascination with grotesqueries like this," he said, pointing at the General.

"Why, because he's different, unusual, one of a kind, sir."

"He is abhorrent. In my country, he would have been fed to the crocodiles at birth. Such creatures bring bad luck."

"Well, sir, he has brought nothing but luck, not to mention heartfelt companionship, to me."

Biniam Sahle sighed and shook his head. "Luck changes. You should be wary of him."

With that the man stepped away and worked his way back among the guests, who were now applauding as General Tom Thumb completed his performance with a comical march across the room as Napoleon Bonaparte.

When the applause died away, Barnum moved to the center of the room, arms raised to get everyone's attention. "That, ladies and gentlemen, was just a taste of the performance — and wonders — you will see at a show I plan to stage in theatre in the coming days."

"More wonders than this marvelous little man?" said the Baroness.

"No one and no *thing* is more wondrous than General Tom Thumb, but I have found a new attraction that I am sure will intrigue and delight you."

"What then?" said the baroness.

"Why, nothing less than an angel — with *wings!* — from heaven itself, and living right here among you."

Several of the guests, incredulous, began to laugh, prompting Barnum to continue. "I know you are skeptical. I was, too. But I have seen her. She is young and white as the snow, with hair to match and eyes you will never forget, eyes that can look into your very souls. And wings, do not forget her wings. I have examined them and they are as real as the nose on my face. You simply *must* come to see her."

Barnum could not tell whether his words had convinced even a single guest. "In any event, come to the theatre and you will see even more of General Tom Thumb."

This last statement prompted another round of applause and the unhurried departure of the various guests. The Abyssinian was quickly at Barnum's side.

"This attraction, this angel, she is albino?" he said.

Barnum nodded. "Yes, but an albino from heaven."

"There is luck and luck," said Biniam Sahle. "Your little man is bad luck, but an albino, that is different. We still feed them to the crocodiles, but we save their hands and heads, which are magic and impart luck and good fortune to the person who has them. I will come to this performance. I will see your angel."

With that, the man turned and walked away.

Barnum stood there, shaking his head as the General walked up.

"What's wrong?" said the General.

Barnum watched as the Abyssinian said his farewells to the baroness and made his way out of the room. "That man there, the Abyssinian."

"So?"

"Nothing, really. Just a strange man."

"Shall we go, then? I am beyond hungry."

"Yes, me too. Why, I'm as hungry as a crocodile."

7

Tom Partly's Traveling Freak Show, a Field in Greenwich, June 6, 1844.

The wagon ride back to Greenwich had taken longer than expected, Tom Partly having developed a thirst requiring nothing less than drinking the night away at a public house, leaving Lily to the darkness of the wagon.

So it was near midday of the next day when the wagon finally rolled into the field and took its place among the other freak shows. Lily put her hands over her eyes to avoid the blinding light she knew would come as Partly swung the wagon doors open and cursed at her.

"Bollocks, what a mess!"

She was still naked, her face and chest red with dried blood.

"Enku," he shouted. "Get your white little arse over here and clean up this little bitch!"

Enku Hassan, a middle-aged Abyssinian albino known in the show as Walla-Walla, the White Witch of Wongo-Bongo, appeared beside Partly and smiled up at Lily. "Oh, child, have we had a bird?"

Enku had seen this so many times. Despite trying her best to teach Lily how to eat cooked food, the girl just preferred to rip hens apart with her teeth. It was frightening for most people to see, the way she could transform her face into a teeth-filled snout, and so Partly had soon made it part of the act, handing her a hen whenever he wanted to scatter the crowd.

Lily smiled back and nodded.

"Get her clean," said Partly, turning away. "The crowds will be here soon enough."

Enku watched him walk away, then turned and climbed into the wagon to release Lily from her chains. "We must kill that man one day," she said, knowing that saying the words were as close as she would ever come to doing the deed. He owned her, and that was that. And besides, she was now too old to consider any other kind of life.

She was a small woman, not quite five-feet tall, and reed thin. Her features—small eyes, flat nose, wide head, and low brow—were like any other Abyssinian, but washed white by albinism. If she had been allowed to dress as an Abyssinian woman, she would have been dressed in a large wide sack chemise, tied off at the waist by a rag. Over that she would have worn what looked like a dirty sheet with a hole in the center, which would have been draped over her head, the cloth falling front and back to the ground. Large black sticks would have been poked through each ear and she would have worn a string of blue beads around her neck. Her hair would have been teased into long curls, which would have glistened from rancid butter.

But she was Walla-Walla, the White Witch of Wongo-Bongo, and must by needs dress like a true Wongo-Bongoin, which in Tom Partly's mind involved a red loincloth and a matching strap of cloth over her small breasts, all designed to show more of her pale skin. Her hair was teased into a pale explosion. Random streaks of blue and red paint over her body completed the fearsome image of Walla-Walla.

"Yes, we must kill him one day," she repeated.

Lily smiled. "You say that every day."

"I know, child. I know. Sometimes it helps, and sometimes it does not. Perhaps you will be the one to do it."

"Why would I do that?"

Enku rolled her eyes. "Child, how many times must I remind you that you are a prisoner here? Or that you are more powerful than you realize. We must pick a time and set you free."

"But this is all I have known, and besides, how could I ever leave you?"

Enku shook her head. "Child, why do you think I teach you to read and write?"

Lily had heard those words almost every day, and provided the answer. "So I can move freely in the world."

"Yes, you can, you can."

"I do not know. It is not so bad, this life. I have you—and fresh chickens!"

Enku laughed. "You and your chickens."

Lily watched as Enku's laugh turned to a frown.

"What?" said Lily.

"I have seen the way that man looks at you. He is biding his time, waiting for you to flower. We must plan, we must plan. I will not let that man have you."

"Would you come with me?"

"No, child. I am too old and have no other place to go in this world. Have you not seen how the people laugh at me?"

"Then I will stay, too."

"Child, child, child. A time of great danger is coming, and you must be free."

"People will laugh at me, too."

Enku shook her head vigorously. "No, you have beauty and power, magic even. You are pale like me, yes, but with the right clothes, you could live among them and be free of that man forever."

Lily could not imagine being without Enku, the woman who had raised her these past ten years, but she didn't want to upset her, either. "I will think about it."

"Good, now let us get you to the stream and clean you up."

Enku studied her as they walked across the field. She was growing larger, more muscular. Each day she came closer and closer to flight. *One day, this little girl will unleash her power*, Enku thought, *and nothing and no one will stand in her way.*

She could not help but smile.

8

Port Famine, Strait of Magellan, February 6, 1834.

Three straight days of torrential rain had kept Darwin on board the *Beagle*, but by the morning of 6 February, the weather had finally cleared enough for them to proceed to Mount Tarn. He and his companions, Rowlett and Martens, along with his assistant, Syms Covington, set off early, just before dawn, and for the next two hours made their way up the mountain through a desolate landscape of deep ravines, fallen, moldering tree trunks, stunted trees, and patches of snow, all while piercingly cold gale winds slowed them at every step.

Then, quite suddenly, a guanaco ran across their path, Rowlett, Martens, and Covington giving chase, firing on the run. Darwin pressed on. From time to time he could hear additional shots, always from farther away. And then, about halfway up the mountain, he spotted what appeared to be a cave. A plume of smoke was rising from it and swirling away in the wind.

9

The Royal Pavilion Theatre, White Chapel Road, Mile End, London, June 10, 1844.

General Tom Thumb strutted across the wide, empty stage, the sound of his boot heels echoing throughout the cavernous hall.

"This will do," he shouted. "This will do!"

Indeed, thought P. T. Barnum. He had not seen the likes of this theatre, from its large stage framed by tall Corinthian columns, to its many rows of seats, to the boxes that seemed to reach to the very heavens. And centered above it all a chandelier almost beyond imagining.

He turned to the stage manager. "Why, I could make a fortune just by showing this chandelier."

The stage manager couldn't have cared less. "So, have you an interest in booking the theatre?"

Barnum liked a man who got down to business. "A question or two, if you don't mind, sir."

"Have at it, then."

"How many people can it accommodate?"

"Three thousand seated, a few more hundred standing, if it comes to that."

"Oh, I expect it will come to that," said Barnum. "And how much to rent the theatre for the night?"

"It varies, but I'm not the one to answer that question."

"What? I thought you were the man in charge."

The stage manager shrugged. "I am, but only after you have booked. You will have to talk to the theatre owner about the rent and the split."

"And when could you arrange that meeting?"

The man pulled a small scrap of paper out of his pocket. "Let me see. Looks like he will be here at two of the clock on the afternoon of tomorrow."

"Excellent. Please advise him that I shall return at said time to parlay with him."

"Very well, sir," said the stage manager, who turned on his heels and walked toward a small door at the back of the stage.

Barnum took one more look around, then called out to the General. "Come, our carriage awaits. Time for you to meet our new attraction."

The General started walking toward Barnum, then suddenly stopped and slammed his boot down hard just to hear the echoes. "This is wonderful, wonderful!"

10

Mount Tarn, Port Famine, Strait of Magellan, February 6, 1834.

Darwin approached the cave cautiously. He didn't want to alarm anyone inside, so he called out in as friendly a tone as he could manage.

Silence.

He called out again, but still there was no response.

He moved closer and peered into the cave, where he saw a young man, pale as a ghost, sitting before a small fire. The man beckoned him in with a wave of his hand, which Darwin noticed had fingernails so long they curled back on each other.

Without a word, the man motioned for Darwin to sit opposite him, the fire between them. As his eyes adjusted to the light, Darwin could finally make out the face and features of this extraordinary young man.

He was clearly a Chinaman, and judging from his near-red eyes and long white-blond hair and beard, one afflicted with that condition that makes a man near devoid of color in every way.

He was dressed head to toe in guanaco skins, but not after the loose fashion of the Fuegian savages and their seal skin capes. His clothing appeared to have been made by a fine tailor, one who might do good business in London.

The man cleared his throat as if he had not spoken a word in months and smiled at Darwin "You are from the ship?"

The words came out haltingly at first but flowed more freely once he had become accustomed to speaking English, which was clearly not his primary language.

"Has my friend Captain Stokes had a change of heart after so many years?" the man said.

His words startled Darwin to the core, and it took a few moments for him to collect himself.

"Is something the matter?" the man said.

"No, I mean yes. Mr. Stokes is dead. Shot himself some years ago, right in this harbor."

The man seemed visibly shaken. "I did not know this, and it saddens me to hear it." He shook his head. "But he was a nervous man and I fear I have had a part in his death."

He reached across the fire and offered Darwin his hand.

"I am Zhao Yu," he said, "Guardian of the White Dragon on the sixth voyage of the treasure fleet, and humble servant of Emperor Zhu Di, may he forever reign in life and memory."

Darwin gulped. *Dragon?*

11

Tom Partly's Traveling Freak Show, a Field in Greenwich, June 10, 1844.

Tom Partly could tell by the elegance of the approaching carriage that his visitor would be none other than Mr. P. T. Barnum, but he was shocked to near senseless when the first person out of the carriage was a tiny man, the likes of which he had never seen before. He had seen dwarves, certainly, but this tiny man was perfectly proportioned, as if he had been shrunk in the wash.

Partly recovered quickly as he saw Mr. Barnum step down from the carriage, his hand extended in greeting. "Good day, sir."

"And a good day to you, Mr. Partly," said Barnum, glancing around at the train of penny-show vans, all brightly painted with images and bold exhortations about the amazing worth of their shows. The closest van was Tom Partly's, which featured his once former top attraction, the so-called white witch.

Barnum looked down the line to the next van, which had a large pictorial sign of giantesses, a white Negro, albino girls, a learned pig, big snakes, and so on. A man standing in front of the van caught sight of him and the General and raced over.

"What say you, mister? Are you not the very man who hired Randall the Giant for America, and you shows this little man here, the amazing Tom Thumb?"

"I am indeed, sir," said Barnum with a quick bow.

"Why, then, sir, for just sixpence, you can see my amazing show, which will startle and boggle, I am sure."

Barnum laughed at the six-time markup. "Why, it must be quite a show at that price."

The man started to answer, but a bevy of other showmen had surrounded them, and had their own shows to sell and more than a few rich comments about the worth of General Tom Thumb.

"I know three dwarfs what is better twelve times than this little man here," said one.

"I concur," said another, "long as Melia Patton lives, Tom Thumb is not worth so much as a breath."

"Now wait," said a third man. "I give your Tom Thumb here his due, but his 'vantage as I sees it is he can chaff so well, like a man. But I can learn my Dick Swift in short order so he can out-chaff Tom Thumb."

"Makes no matter," said a fourth man. "It is more than chaff and banter, for as you all know, Tom has the name, and the name is everything. Tom Thumb couldn't never shine in my van 'long side a half dozen dwarfs I know, if this Yankee hadn't bamboozled the Baroness Rothschild."

"Yes, yes, that's the ticket," said a fifth man. "Soon, no doubt, he shall perform for the queen — she loves all things *foreign* — and we shall all be as worthless as Old Jake's wax-works."

"What!" shouted none other than Old Jake. "Me beautiful wax-works is beyond compare."

As the other men surrounded Old Jake to offer their opinions, Barnum grabbed Partly and the General and quickly retreated to an area behind Partly's van, where they could talk without interruption.

"You sees what I have to put up with every day?" said Partly.

Barnum chuckled. "A showman's life, eh? Nothing better, sir, nothing better. Now, without further ado, where might we find my angel? Tom has a mind to see her for himself."

"Yes," said the General. "Where is this so-called act?"

Partly pointed to a cage covered by a heavy tarp. "They's here, the girl and her companion, Walla-Walla."

Partly tugged the tarp off with a flourish, surprising Lily to the point that she fluttered her wings and bared her sharp teeth. The other albino reached out to calm her, and the girl was quickly back to normal, no more than an albino girl in rags.

General Tom Thumb just stood there, mouth agape for some seconds before finally whistling through his teeth. "Oh, my."

"Did I not tell you, Tom? A bona fide first-rate attraction, one worthy to stand with you on the same stage."

The General looked worried. "But not at the same time, surely?"

"No, of course not," said Barnum. "A completely separate act, with you as top billing, never you worry about that."

The General seemed relieved. "What about the other one, this Walla-Walla?"

"She is of no interest," said Barnum.

"Hold, sir," said Partly. "To has one is to has the other, for your angel will not be separated from her."

Barnum shook his head, then nodded. "A companion, then, but not an act."

"Yes, a companion. She calms her, as you see."

Barnum removed his top hat and wiped a handkerchief across his pate. "Well, then, let's get down to it. Would you take a hundred pounds for the two of them?"

Partly laughed. "Our agreement was for rental, one show at a time. I shall not take a hundred, when thousands may be on the table."

Barnum nodded. "I only seek to save you from the downside. It could be that no one will like the act or that something might go wrong during her first performance. She's so new to this, you see."

"Now, see here, Mr. Barnum, I knows my Lily, and she knows what to do, and I knows my lines, and she will be heavily chained, so there will be no hitch in our performance."

"I see," said Barnum. "I meet with the theatre owner on the morrow. Once I have his terms, we can discuss your terms. Come, General, time to return to Grafton Street."

Partly watched them walk away and make their way through the crowd of showmen blocking the carriage. Soon, though, the horses were drawing them away, some showmen trotting behind, shouting out criticism and generally unkind words.

Enku interrupted him. "She would like a chicken."

12

Port Famine, Strait of Magellan, February 6, 1834, Evening.

FitzRoy took a sip of his tea and glanced over at Darwin, who sat opposite him, slumped in his chair, seemingly deep in thought.

"My dear fellow, you look exhausted."

Oh, you have no idea, Darwin thought. He looked up and reached for his cup of tea. "Admittedly, sir, it was quite a day."

"All that climbing?"

"Yes."

"And no guanaco to show for it."

"It was the fastest I have ever seen."

FitzRoy set down his cup. "Pity, I was so looking forward to a good meal, recompense for our efforts in this weather."

"Again, my apologies."

FitzRoy drummed his fingers on the table. "So, then, am I to assume that you found no majestic winged bird?"

Darwin thought back to the cave and the fantastical story told to him by that strange man, Zhao Yu, a story of an ill-fated voyage, a shipwreck, and an impossible cargo. And *dragons!* The man was mad.

Darwin shook his head. "Indeed, I did not."

"So that is an end to it, this fantasy of yours?"

"Yes, sir. Still, I saw some geological specimens I would like to collect there tomorrow. I lacked the necessary tools today, so if you do not mind . . ."

FitzRoy was pleased. "Of course, of course, Philos, by all means take another day to explore."

Darwin could not wait to get back to the cave and all that he had seen there. He trembled with excitement. "Thank you, sir."

"And perhaps a guanaco is in our future after all?"

"It is devoutly to be wished, sir."

13

The Royal Pavilion Theatre, White Chapel Road, Mile End, London, June 11, 1844.

There was no doubt that General Tom Thumb loved the theatre, especially the vast stage of the Royal Pavilion. No sooner had he and Barnum stepped on the stage than the little man proceeded to dance and march across it, in the direction of three men standing at its center.

Barnum recognized the stage manager immediately, but the other two gentlemen were unknown. Presumably, one was the theatre owner. If he had to guess, he would have said the shorter, rounder one, who looked like someone used to counting money. The other man, by contrast, as well dressed as he was, looked more like a man you'd want to accompany you through a dark alley, so tall and wide was he, with a menacing aspect.

As Barnum and the General approached, the stage manager stepped forward. "Ah, Mr. Barnum, may I introduce Mr. Niles Crawford, owner-proprietor of this establishment."

The shorter man extended his hand in greeting. "A pleasure, sir."

"Likewise," said Barnum. "And this other gentleman here?"

Crawford glanced briefly at the other man, who nodded back, then said, "An *associate*. If our negotiations go well, I will introduce you more formally."

With that, Crawford motioned Barnum to a small table stage left, where they took chairs opposite one another. The stage manager quickly disappeared backstage, while the tall gentleman amused himself by watching the General's antics, which he seemed to thoroughly enjoy.

Crawford got right to the point. "How many acts, and your estimated run time." His words came out more as a demand than a question.

"Just two," said Barnum. "A new act involving an angelic young girl, followed by General Tom Thumb. I would expect the run time, in total, to be about two hours, perhaps somewhat less."

Crawford drummed his fingers on the table as if he were performing a difficult problem in arithmetic. "And the draw?"

"I would expect a full house, perhaps even standing room only."

Crawford glanced over at the General. "For that little man?"

"Indeed," said Barnum, glancing over at the tall man, who was clapping his hands to the beat of the General's march. "He already has a large following, particularly among the lords and ladies. You may expect the Baroness Rothschild to attend, and . . ."

He paused for effect. "And," he continued, "perhaps the *queen* herself."

The man beamed. "Well, then, here are my terms. Firstly, a one-time payment of ten pounds."

Barnum nodded.

"Secondly, an admission fee of thruppence for the gallery, a shilling for the lower boxes or stalls, and three shillings for the elevated boxes, all split seventy on the cent for you, and thirty for me."

"A moment," said Barnum, pulling a roughly folded piece of paper from his waistcoat, which included a chart of his own construction showing the myriad denominations in the most confusing currency in the world: farthings, pence, shillings, florins, crowns, sovereigns—all made even more difficult to parse out because of their nicknames, from joeys to tanners to bobs to cartwheels to groats.

"So," continued Barnum, "what does that come to for a full house?"

Crawford looked heavenward for guidance, his eyes twitching with each calculation. Thirty lower boxes and stalls at a shilling per, plus 12 upper boxes at 3 shillings per, plus near three thousand gallery seats at a thruppence per. "That would make about forty pounds, more or less.

•   •   •

The figure seemed low for an act of General Tom Thumb's stature, not to mention the intrigue provided by his angel.

"Well, then," said Barnum. "Let's double those numbers."

Crawford sat back in his chair, clearly amazed. "Double? No one gets those kind of prices. It will damp down the take."

"No," said Barnum. "At the higher price, the people will come, especially the royals and the curious, expecting something of great value. And value, sir, is what I always deliver."

Crawford shook his head vigorously. "I would then require a larger portion."

Barnum nodded. "Sixty-five, thirty-five, then."

Crawford sighed, shaking his head all the while. "I still worry about the value, Mr. Barnum. Would you be agreeable if I add a feature at the end of the show? I have a new play, you see, called a "Child of the Wave."

Barnum shook his head. "Add what you like at the end, but first my angel and then my Tom."

"All right, done, but know this. Those prices will also attract pickpockets. I must insist on security, inside and outside the theatre, the expense to be shared equally."

"And how would that work, exactly?" said Barnum.

"Ah," said Crawford, "that would be where Mr. Field would come in."

He motioned Barnum to his feet and they proceeded across the stage, where the large man was laughing and slapping his knees at the General's performance.

Crawford grabbed him by the arm to get his attention, and the man's demeanor changed in an instant, going from mirth to wariness. Barnum fully expected the man to strike out in anger, so menacing was his look.

Crawford let go of Field's arm and took a step back. "Mr. Barnum, may I present Mr. Charles Field, one of our fine policemen."

Field bowed and offered his meaty hand. "That is *Inspector* Charles Frederick Field of the Detective, in Whitehall, the Great Scotland Yard."

Barnum took his hand, surprised at the firmness of the man's grip. "The Detective?"

"Yes," said Field. "No uniform, you see. Let's me proceed at will and discover what needs to be discovered. Discreetly."

"I see," said Barnum.

Up close, the man was even more imposing. He was as tall as Barnum, but thicker in every direction, though the weight did not suggest corpulence. He was middle-aged from the look of him, but carried himself like a younger man. His eyes were moist and penetrating, even knowing, and his voice was low and husky. Most peculiarly, he had the odd habit of waving his fat forefinger in front of his face as a way to both intimidate the listener and accent every spoken word. It almost seemed he was fencing with his finger.

"And here is what *I* see, Mr. Barnum," he said, waving his finger in front of Barnum's nose. "I see a man who expects the best for a fair price, do I not?"

Barnum nodded.

"I also see a tiny person here, a child of no more than seven if I had to guess."

"Thirteen," said Barnum.

Field held his forefinger motionless in front of Barnum's face, than twirled it away to point at the General. "Me and Mrs. Field know children, loves children, because the lord has not blessed us with any. So it is that we admire them so, know them so well. No, this is a child of seven, or certainly no more than eight. And the point is, the point is, Mr. Barnum, this lad needs protection, protection of the highest value and enforcement."

"And you aim to provide it, no doubt," said Barnum.

"I do, sir. You are a quick study, certainly, for that is exactly what I propose, me and my men, to protect you and this fine lad from pickers and smashers. I knows them and more importantly, they knows *me*." He accented this last point with a jab of his forefinger, which Barnum was beginning to find annoying in the extreme. Barnum also had the impression that people high and low would melt away in the wake of this man and his chubby finger.

"And what is your fee?" said Barnum.

"A crown for me, and one bob each for my twelve men."

Crawford stepped in. "That's extremely fair, Mr. Barnum. I can vouch for the quality of this man's service."

Barnum nodded. "Very well, we have a deal, Mr. Field."

Field gave a quick bow, then jabbed a finger toward Barnum. "You shall not be disappointed, sir. I guarantee it."

14

Mount Tarn, Port Famine, Strait of Magellan, February 7, 1834.

As Darwin climbed Mount Tarn, headed back to the cave of the strange Chinaman, Zhao Yu, he reflected on the bizarre story the man had told him and the promise of an unspecified "natural specimen" for Darwin to study.

As he walked, he kept his eyes open for the large bird he knew must be at the heart of the superstitious Fuegian's myth of a dragon-man, a story professed to be true by Zhao Yu, who claimed to be the beast's father.

Darwin shook his head. Such a species flew in the face of all he and the scientific world knew about nature. It was just not possible. Still, the man had insisted that a combination of natural acts had created a situation ripe for new laws, and new species.

Darwin chuckled to himself. It was so ridiculous, this man's claim that first, there were dragons in the world, and second, that a small barnacle had set everything in motion to create the man's children, one born live—his son and the source of the myth among the Fuegians—and one unborn and dead within a "dragon's egg."

And yet the man had produced no son and no egg. His story was pure fabrication in every respect, for what purpose, Darwin could only guess.

He could smell the smoke before he saw it, and was soon within the cave, sitting opposite Zhao Yu, skeptical about what might come next, yet thankful to be out of the cold.

As promised, Darwin had brought along a package of tea and a small sack. Zhao Yu took both and, in silence, began to prepare tea, which he served in small cups he had clearly crafted from the local clay.

"You are a doubter," said Zhao Yu, handing him a cup of tea. "I saw that from the first."

Darwin took a tentative sip—it was wonderful!—and shook his head. "No, I am a man of science. Claims mean nothing until they are proved."

"And you claim my son is not real," said Zhao Yu, setting his own cup aside.

"I see no son, only a story of a son."

Zhao Yu smiled. "I cannot show you a son who has already flown to other shores."

"Indeed."

"So we are at what you call an impasse."

"Yes, I guess we are."

Zhao Yu reached behind him and pulled out a bundle covered by a small guanaco pelt. "Consider this, then."

Zhao Yu pulled the pelt away, revealing a large egg, similar in size to an ostrich egg, yet different in color and shape, and thoroughly covered in the strangest barnacles Darwin had ever seen.

Darwin reached out for it, but Zhao Yu pulled it back. "First, a suggestion. What you see here is my other child, born still in this egg many years ago. I will not burden you further with the story I have already told you about how this barnacle-encrusted egg came to be, or how the dragon egg entrusted to me by the emperor came to be covered in these same barnacles, the effect of which was to drive it mad. I know you do not believe my story."

Darwin nodded.

"But here is something *real*, something you can study, and ultimately confirm what I have told you. These are the same barnacles that appeared on the egg entrusted to me by the emperor. Take the egg back with you to your homeland, where you will have time to study it in detail. I am sure that you will not only discover a poorly formed man-dragon—my child—inside, you will also see how this barnacle has insinuated itself through the shell of the egg, and by whatever process, has mutated what lies within. That is my suggestion, my challenge to you. Take it home, study it, and then decide what is real and what is not."

With that, he slipped the egg into the sack and handed it over to Darwin.

"I will do as you say," said Darwin, already entranced by the barnacles and the egg itself.

Zhao Yu bowed. "Our meeting is at an end."

The man waited until Darwin had left the cave before picking up his cup and sipping his now-cold tea.

He chuckled to himself. Darwin had taken the bait, and now his second child, near ready to hatch, was on its way to England.

He tossed out the tea and poured a second cup, steaming hot.

15

The Royal Pavilion Theatre, White Chapel Road, Mile End, London, Tuesday Evening, June 18, 1844.

Barnum peeked through the curtains and did a little jig. "Come here, Mr. Crawford, and behold our work!"

Crawford came over and dutifully obeyed. "A full house."

"You seem not pleased."

"Such a crowd means two things, Mr. Barnum: money and *trouble*."

"Pah," said Barnum. "You and I have assured the first, and Mr. Field shall prevent the second."

Crawford shrugged in a way that suggested he was not quite sure how the evening would go. "Let us hope. Now, I must to the box office to begin the final count."

Barnum watched him disappear through a small door stage right, then turned back to peer through a gap in the curtains.

The crowd was a mix of all classes, from the poor to the very rich, including many lords and ladies, and buzzing with excitement from the playbill that suggested they would be seeing a very angel this evening, as well as the amazing General Tom Thumb.

He could see the Rothschilds in an elevated box in the second tier, just to the left of the stage, giving them a perfect vantage point to see the act, and Lily's wings, unfold. A balding, beetle-browed gentleman and his comely wife sat in the box just below the Rothschilds, but although she was finely dressed in a royal blue gown, his frumpy brown waistcoat could not place them in the noble class, as was the case with the royals in the remaining elevated boxes. The lower boxes and even the gallery contained an overflow of royals who had apparently waited too long to buy their tickets.

Three people in the gallery stood out: none other than the Abyssinian envoy, Biniam Sahle, whose attention seemed to be focused not on the stage, but on a tall, burly man in black sitting in the front row, center stage, a man who was clearly an albino, his pale skin and hair clear giveaways, as were his deeply shaded glasses, which gave him a menacing air; and Inspector Field of the Detective, who was watching both of them closely from his vantage point along the far aisle to the right of the stage, his cudgel tapping slowly in his palm. If trouble came, he would be ready.

Barnum closed the curtains and looked back at Mr. Partly and Lily, who had moved into position, and then to Enku, who stood apart, just offstage, looking nervous. He turned his attention back to his performers.

"You will be wonderful," said Barnum. "Wonderful!"

16

Port Famine, Strait of Magellan, February 7, 1834, Evening.

FitzRoy stabbed a piece of meat with a fork and put it in his mouth. "Ah, that's better, don't you think? Not beef, of course, but it will do."

Darwin nodded. He had barely touched the roasted guanaco. His stomach was churning from seasickness and his head was spinning over the events of the day. He couldn't wait to get back to the small cabin he shared with two other crewmen, settle in at the chart table, and record everything he had seen and heard the past two days.

"You look a little green, Philos. The usual?"

"Yes, it is always worse when I first come back onboard, even in seas as relatively calm as Port Famine."

FitzRoy took another bite. "Well, I am happy to have the guanaco, but I am sorry your excursion was otherwise unproductive."

"Not totally, sir. I did find an interesting barnacle."

FitzRoy put down his fork. "A barnacle, you say. On a mountain?"

"It is not unusual. In fact, there is a theory that—"

FitzRoy slapped his knee. "I nearly forgot. I meant to tell you this story yesterday, when you came back so disappointed about not finding that so-called dragon." He couldn't help laughing.

"Oh?"

"Your mention of barnacles brought it all back to me. Anyway, if you want to see a true monster, a true wonder, you may have your chance not many months from now when we sail into the Pacific."

Darwin looked puzzled. "What kind of monster?"

"A gigantic white whale, a beast that dwarfs this ship. They call him Mocha Dick, after the island of Mocha, where he was first spotted some years ago. He is supposedly incredibly powerful, and has stove or harassed many a ship. And to the point about the barnacles, his entire head is said to be encrusted with them. They are said to have driven him quite mad. At any rate, if we see him, I am sure we will have quite a story to tell."

Darwin felt a chill go up his spine. *Oh, my God.*

17

Port Famine, Strait of Magellan, February 7, 1834, Late Evening.

Darwin excused himself and made his way back to the poop cabin he shared with a surveyor and a midshipman, both of whom were already asleep, the surveyor in a bunk just outside the cabin and the midshipman in a hammock above the chart table, where Darwin's hammock was also strung. The whole place smelled of salt and sweat.

The cabin was barely ten feet by ten feet, with a large chart table in the center, leaving barely enough room to walk around it. The walls were lined with shelves for the ship's library of nearly 300 books and pamphlets, including Darwin's own, and the rest of the space was crammed with a small oven for heat, a wash-stand, a chest of drawers, an instrument cabinet, and a water closet. To make things even more cramped, the mizzen mast ran straight through the cabin from floor to ceiling. The three had come to call it "the pole of frivolity," so comical were their interactions to move about the cabin without interfering with one another.

Darwin had thought to write more in his journal, but the hammock was just too inviting, and he was exhausted. The journal would have to wait till morning. He pulled off his boots and waistcoat, loosened his cravat, and climbed into the hammock, trying his best not to disturb the midshipman, who was snoring away, as usual. He fell asleep quickly.

•   •   •

After three years at sea, you learn to detect changes in the weather by even the slightest motions of the ship, particularly when you're below deck. Even in his hammock he could tell that a storm was rolling over the harbor, waves slamming into the ship, making it pitch violently. He tried to wake the midshipman, but the man wouldn't budge, so he jumped from his hammock, tugged on his boots, and made his was up to the deck.

FitzRoy was at the helm, and looked terrified as wave after wave crashed onto the deck. When he saw Darwin, he started shouting, but his words were lost in the sound of thunder and crashing waves.

Darwin shouted to him, but FitzRoy just shook his head and pointed to starboard. Darwin turned, and froze. A whale, pale as milk and as massive as a mountain was bearing down on the ship. He turned back to FitzRoy, but he was gone, the wheel spinning back and forth on its own.

And then with a mighty crack the ship was breaking apart, the whale's giant head splitting it in two with one massive blow. Darwin grabbed for the rail to prevent himself from sliding into the churning sea, but as he did, he felt pain shooting through both shoulders and heard the sound of giant wings. Something was lifting him higher and higher into the sky. It shrieked.

"Mr. Darwin, Mr. Darwin, wake up!"

Darwin startled awake. The midshipman was standing over him. "What? What!"

"You were screaming, sir."

Darwin slumped back in the hammock. "A nightmare."

The surveyor, barely awake, stumbled into the cabin. "What is going on?"

"All over, mate. Mr. Darwin here was having himself a right old nightmare." He turned to Darwin. "Must have been something the way you were carrying on. Here, take this cloth. You are right soaked through."

Darwin took the cloth and wiped the sweat from his face. "I am indeed sorry. I did not mean to wake you."

"Not a problem, sir, start of my watch, anyway. Are you going to be okay?"

Darwin nodded. "Yes," he said. *No*, he thought.

Darwin waited until they had left, and lit a lamp. The nightmare seemed to energize him. Time to write down all that he had seen and heard in the Cave of Zhao Yu.

He set to work, writing through the night and greeting dawn still hunched over the chart table, penning a letter to his dear friend and mentor, Professor John Stevens Henslow.

My Dear Henslow

If you are reading this, I am either quite dead or, alternatively, standing next to you, bursting with excitement. — If neither, than surely I am in Bedlam, for my story alone. In any case, it is time to explain the events & discoveries of 6-7 February 1834, & decide what should be done with the enclosed journal, egg, & barnacles. Particularly the barnacles, some of which are unlike anything I have ever seen before, & worthy of extensive study alone. I pray you followed my instructions & secreted away this small cask, so that its contents remained safe & secure in my absence. — You will also note that I have included a similar letter to my sisters in the event you decide to share the journal with them after my death. I wanted to put their minds at ease that I was not — am not — void of my senses, although upon reading my journal, I can certainly appreciate how anyone might think otherwise & send me Bedlam bound. — Given these discoveries, I cannot decide whether to continue on this voyage or find speedy transport home. — I am in a quandary, but you now know which decision I have taken. — I put all my trust & faith in you, as I have done these many years.

Till then believe me, my dear Henslow; Yours very truly obliged,
–Chas Darwin

Please break this news gently to my sisters, if circumstances so warrant.

He blotted the document dry, then set it atop his "dragon journal," wrapping the letters and the little book in oil cloth before placing them in a small cask containing the barnacle-encrusted egg. The HMS *Basenthwaite* was due in port on the morrow and would assure its safe passage to Liverpool and then on to Professor Henslow in London.

Darwin thought to sleep, but now released from the focus of writing, his head and stomach rebelled once more, sending him quickly on deck to make another offering to the sea.

PART TWO

I have been asked many times about my earliest memory, whether it was my first encounter with Enku or Mr. Partly, or sometime later. Most are surprised when I tell them I have memories of floating in darkness, as if on a midnight sea, and sounds, so many sounds! Splashing, shouting, creaking, flapping, knocking, all ending with a crashing noise, blinding light, unbearable cold, and the feel of wet grass. That, and the smell of something I later learned was rum.

– Lily, *Interview with the Dragon* (excerpt)

18

Brunswick Docks, Liverpool, June 13, 1834, Morning.

Slint and Sloth sat in the shade, sharing a meat pie and watching the men of two ships, a brig named *Basenthwaite* and a barque named the *Duchess of Clarence*, unload their cargo.

The morning had not progressed all that well for Slint and Sloth, their only success being an artful picking of a fine gentleman, only to find he'd been carrying barely enough for the meager pie, which was not all that tasty. Or perhaps it was just the foul dock smells — fish rotting in the summer sun — that made them think so.

"Whatcha thinkin', Mr. Sloth?"

Sloth finished chewing the last bit, then screwed up his face and spat. "Not much in the way of gentlemen about is what I see. Maybe something from the ships?"

Slint peered at the ships. The men of the *Basenthwaite*, all Englishmen, were unloading mostly boxes and barrels, some large, some small. The crew of the *Duchess of Clarence*, mostly Chinamen, odd looking little men to Slint's mind, had their share of barrels, but the baggage and packages of tea caught his eye.

"I am thinking baggage and tea, Mr. Sloth. The gypsy king has a fancy for tea, I hear, and I could use some new clothes."

Sloth laughed. "Aye, Mr. Slint, you are in dear need of a tailor and a bit of a wash. Have I told you you smell like a horse?"

"You have indeed, sir, and have I told you that you smell like a ripe hog bloating in the sun?"

"Most definitely, sir, we are barnyard brothers, are we not?"

Slint cackled and raised a finger into the air, as if he were a speechifying actor. "And who more deserving of some finery, Mr. Sloth?"

"Why, sir," said Sloth, thumping a hand on his chest. "I see no other worthies but us."

They both laughed, punching at each other's shoulders. Slint rose to his feet. "Well, sir, shall we be about it?"

Sloth started to rise, then pulled Slint back to the ground. "Look over there," he said, pointing.

Slint looked on in wonder at a tall young man standing on the gangplank of the *Duchess of Clarence*. He was dressed all in red save for his hat, some shiny fabric that caught the light of the early morning sun and made the man appear to glow. His hat, which appeared to be made of dried grass or some such, looked like some sort of pointy mushroom had been placed on his head. He peered out at the world through orange spectacles. But none of that was what made Slint's mouth drop open. The man was as white as a ghost, with near-white hair falling to his shoulders.

"Mother of God!" said Slint. "Can he really be Chinese? He be white as gull shit."

Sloth nodded. "I dare say, Mr. Slint. Belongs in a freak show, he does. I saw one of them once. Scary. Beady red eyes. Not natural."

Slint cocked his head and looked back and forth between the man on the gangplank and Sloth, as if he were developing a plan, but the bubble of it had not yet surfaced.

"What?" said Sloth, recognizing Slint's screwed up face for what it was, a plan in the mixin' bowl, which usually spelled trouble.

Slint scratched his chin. "I be thinkin', Mr. Sloth, as I have a mind to do now and again. And I am thinkin' mayhap we drop a hammer on him. Get good money, I bet."

Sloth shook his head emphatically. "Not a chance, Mr. Slint. They is unlucky. I hear you touch one, you die."

"Just by touching?"

"Aye, I hear you drop right down, foam at the mouth like an ailing hound, and die."

Slint sniffed and tapped a finger on the side of his nose. "Well, then, Mr. Sloth, perhaps a barrel or two from the other ship?"

Sloth beamed. "I like the way you think, sir. I truly like the way you think. *When* you think, I mean."

Slint glowered at him.

19

Brunswick Docks, Liverpool, June 13, 1834, Morning.

Bai Li, special envoy of the emperor, stood on the gangplank of the *Duchess of Clarence* and weighed whether to go ashore immediately or wait for his assistant, Huang Peng, who among other faults had no appreciation for the movement of time, one of the rotten fruits of near immortality.

He adjusted his amber spectacles and glanced back and forth at the hustle and bustle of life on the docks. *Such dirty foul creatures. And they say they are the civilized ones? Absurd.*

Two of these creatures seemed to epitomize how foul the English were. They were standing in front of a warehouse, clothed in near rags, slapping at each other like fools, and filthy dirty from head to foot. He glanced around to see if Huang Peng was anywhere in sight. Nothing. *This will not go well*, he thought.

Shouts on the dock caught his attention. The two men, both with barrels on each of their shoulders, were now running for their lives with several dock workers in pursuit. *Time to get away from this ship and these docks.*

The voyage from China to Liverpool, the first tea shipment to Liverpool not under the banner of the East India Company, had been mostly uneventful, the Chinese crew sailing the unfamiliar vessel effortlessly. His instructions were clear. He was to find lodgings for himself, Huang Peng, and thirty settlers—men, women, and children—and use Liverpool as a base for their mission.

Li had his doubts about the emperor's plan, but a mission was a mission. It just meant he'd probably be in England a long, long time. *With people like these?* He shuddered.

He heard the heavy, unmistakable thumps of Huang Peng walking up behind him and setting down their bags.

"You are late, again," he said, turning.

Where Bai Li was tall, heavily muscled, and graceful, Huang Peng was short, fat, and lumbering. Bai Li regretted agreeing to take him along. He would never make an effective envoy, unless it involved food or slicing a person to pieces with his fan, which was always no more than a few inches away from his sweaty face. The fan looked like a large butterfly struggling to be free.

"Sorry," Huang Peng said. "There was food for the taking."

"Are we ready to go?"

"Yes."

"Weapons?"

He pointed to the bags. "Yes."

"Let us go, then." He started down the gangplank, Huang Peng following slowly and grunting under his load.

20

Two miles east of the Brunswick Docks, Liverpool, June 13, 1834, Morning.

Slint and Sloth sat in the shade of a tree, gasping for breath and laughing despite themselves. They had managed to give their pursuers the slip, thanks to some clever changes of direction, all part and parcel to the thieving trade, and clearly well done this day.

"Oh, Mr. Sloth, that were some fine running."

Sloth could barely speak. "Yes," he managed to get out.

Slint slapped the tops of the four small casks they had managed to steal, three sounding about the same, one sounding a bit different, a hollow sort of sound, as if it were nearly empty.

"Let's see what we have, Mr. Sloth."

"Aye." Sloth took a deep breath, grabbed one of the casks, and cackled. "Oh, my dear Mr. Slint, there be rum here!"

"And here and here, Mr. Sloth!"

Sloth beamed. "What a fine day this is, Mr. Slint."

"Indeed, sir, a day for sitting in the shade with a fine libation."

"A what? I thought we hads rum?"

Slint shook his head and rolled his eyes. "Oh, Mr. Sloth, your lack of knowledge still amazes."

Sloth laughed. "Well, I'm full set to amaze as long as there be rum and not this lib-i-ation you speak of."

"They are one and the same, Mr. Sloth, and lucky for us." He looked at the fourth cask. "Now, what have we here?"

Slint pulled the cask over and gave it a little shake. "Well, whatever it is, it rattles a bit."

"What do the label say, Mr. Slint?"

"Whatever it wishes, Mr. Sloth. You know I cannot read."

"Shall we open it, then, and have a look?"

Slint considered the idea and then considered the rum. "This one can wait. Let us have a draught or two of rum and see how the day unfolds, Mr. Sloth."

"Once again, Mr. Slint, I like the way you think."

21

Two miles east of the Brunswick Docks, Liverpool, June 13, 1834, Afternoon.

Sloth was holding on to the grass with all his might, but the world continued to spin, and someone who vaguely reminded him of Slint was screaming and rapping him on the head.

"Sloth, Sloth, Sloth!"

Sloth opened one eye to see if the world was actually spinning, and it was—*fast*. "Sod off!" He closed his eye and continued spinning.

"Sloth, you bastard, you are as drunk as a Blood."

Sloth tried to nod and realized he couldn't quite remember how. And now hands were on his head, lifting him up, fingers prying open his eyes.

"Look for yourself, you fool!"

Sloth forced himself to focus, to slow the spin so he could make sense of the white thing writhing on the ground in front of him. It was making a noise, almost like a purr, but with some hint of a growl, as well.

"Whazit?" he managed and then closed his eyes. *Blessed darkness, healer of lost souls.*

"Well, that is the question, Mr. Sloth, and I have nary an answer. I woke up, and there it was, full busted out of that cask."

Slint poked it with his finger. "Seems to be asleep now. Must have exhausted itself."

Sloth opened his eyes and rubbed his face hard with both hands, trying to rub out some of the effects of the rum. "Let me have a look. It must be *something*, right?"

"I think *thing* might be the right word, Mr. Sloth."

Sloth managed to get up on all fours and peer down at the object in question. "Why it is a baby, is all."

"Yes, but a baby *what*?"

Sloth looked again. The baby had the sweetest face, and— "Mother of God!" He jumped back.

Slint patted him on the back. "A sweet face, yes, and two arms and two legs, but look at those feet. They be more like claws."

"It is a changeling!" shouted Sloth, pulling out his dagger. "We should kill it!"

Slint grabbed Sloth's arm and forced the dagger down. "Nay, Mr. Sloth, nay. We need to tie it up and bag it, so it cannot get away. Then we should take it to the gypsy king. He will pay good money for such a thing."

Sloth shook his head. "But who be king now that Boswell is in his grave?"

Slint shook his head. "Dunno, but a king is a king, right?"

"Maybe," said Sloth. "But you never know, do you, and it is ever so far to Nottinghamshire. How do we keep such a thing alive? And the woods be full of Bos'lls who would slit our throats just for the fun and practice."

Slint nodded. "You have a right point, Mr. Sloth."

They both fell silent, each searching their rum-addled minds for a plan. And then Slint slapped his leg and danced a little jig.

"Why did I not think of this a'fore, Mr. Sloth?" he chortled. "We are not more than a day's walk from that freak show that has been making the rounds. They are going to bloody love this little baby, um, *thing*."

"Oh, Mr. Slint, there be genius 'tween your ears this day."

Slint tugged off the rope around his waist. "Quick then, Mr. Sloth, let us tie it up, bag it, and be away."

"But we have no sack."

"Aye, we do. There was one in the cask, though there be a hole in it now."

Sloth pulled the sack out of the cask and began knotting the end with the hole in it. "No problem, Mr. Slint. I will knot 'er up proper, and we will be on our way. But what about whatever else be in the cask?"

"Nothing but egg shells and what looks like a bundle of books."

"Shall we take 'em?"

Slint considered, but only briefly. "Nay, Mr. Sloth, we have enough to carry with the rum and this thing, and we need to move quickly. No need for the scribblings of learned men."

Sloth shrugged. "All right, words are of no matter to us, anyway."

Slint picked up the thing, now tied up right good, slid it carefully into the sack, and threw it over his shoulder. "Take the rum, Mr. Sloth, and let us be on our way. I know just the place to stop for the night."

"Aye, I was not about to forget the rum." If they were quick enough, perhaps they could get the world spinnin' again by nightfall.

22

The Toad and Fox, Seven Miles East of Liverpool, Evening, June 13, 1834.

Sloth sat next to the fire, breathing in the wood smoke, daubing his cuts with a wet cloth, and sipping a flagon of rum, what was left of the rum they hadn't sold to the proprietor of this fine establishment for a tidy sum. Now they could have a decent meal and reflect on the day, with a rum, a smoke, a soft bed, and gentlemanly conversation befitting their standing as men with coin — maybe even a bath.

"I do not think it meant it," said Sloth. "It is just a baby."

Slint puffed on his pipe. "Mr. Sloth, you are too kind. Did you not see the way it had changed, those eyes, those teeth, those talons, those funny bumps on its forehead, those scales down its back, and a swishy tail and wings to boot? And the look it gave us! Like we would make a right fine meal."

"And where be it now, Mr. Slint?

"After you ran away screaming, I managed to stun it with my fists and wrestle it back into the sack. Then our proprietor was kind enough to provide a sturdy box for a fair price. And a mutton chop to toss in with it. Never heard such sounds, sir."

"Do you think we can still sell it, it being so dangerous and all?"

"A'course. Just makes it more spectacular. Why I can see it now, Mr. Sloth. *Come see the reptile monster and be in fear of your very life!*"

"Looks more like a little dragon to me, Mr. Slint."

"Whatever, mate. The point is, the more terrifying, the more coin we can ask."

"And how far to the freak show?"

"If we set off at first light, we should reach it by midday."

"Shall we to bed, then?"

Slint laughed. "Why, sir, I see there is still rum to be had, so sleep if you wish. Meself will be here by the fire till my flagon be dry."

"Why, sir, twixt rum and sleep, there be no choice. Fill my flagon, sir, and stuff my pipe. There be time before sleep."

23

Two miles east of the Brunswick Docks, Liverpool, June 13, 1834, Dusk.

The man sniffed at the air, hoping to find the scent again, but all he could smell was rum. He picked up the small cask and sniffed at it again. It was definitely her, the sister his father had told him was dead so many years ago. His father had tricked him, and now he would have to deal with this threat. Find her. Kill her.

He lifted his dark spectacles briefly to stare at the ground for other clues, but there were only the egg fragments and a bundle of books wrapped in oil cloth. He gathered them all up and stuffed them back into the broken cask.

The sound of men approaching startled him. He slipped the cask under his black cape and moved quickly into the woods.

24

Five miles south of the Toad and Fox, June 14, 1834, Noon.

It was Slint's turn to hold the wriggling sack that contained the little white beast. Sloth was a few steps ahead, bent over at the waist, huffing and puffing for breath.

"Are we there yet?" said Sloth, looking up at Slint and the sack he held at arm's length. "Should have kept it boxed."

"If we are not soon, I shall take a knife to it, I swear." He tossed the sack on the ground and sat down on the path—you could hardly call it a road—that led to the field where the penny shows were said to be.

"I shall join you in repose," said Sloth, dropping to the ground, thankful to be off his feet, where painful new blisters throbbed unmercifully.

"A moment only," said Slint, "for I hear even now the sound of the penny show and the clink-a-clink of coin soon to be ours."

"Mr. Slint, you has a way with them words."

Slint cupped a hand over his ear and leaned toward a bend in the path. "We is here," he said, scrabbling to his feet. "Just 'round the bend, not a hundred steps."

Sloth got to his feet. "Shall I take the sack, then?"

Slint smiled. "You is a gentleman to do so, sir."

"I's always a gentleman, but more, I does not want you takin' a blade to the babe and lose our well-deserved coin in the bargain."

"Come then," said Slint, moving away.

Sloth grabbed the sack and limped along behind him. *Damnable blisters!*

A hundred steps later and they were just turning the bend, the show wagons coming into view, but still a hundred and a hundred steps away.

Sloth groaned. "Your maths be wrong."

Slint nodded. "So be it, for I can smells gold."

They trudged on, Sloth cursing quietly at the wriggling sack. "Stay, stay, you wildling!"

The proprietors of the first few shows took one look into the sack and backed away in horror. They would have nothing to do with it. But the showman standing in front of a wagon proclaiming the wonders of Walla-Walla, the White Witch of Wongo-Bongo, saw something of value when he peered inside.

"Blimey," he said, "that be a right wonder."

Slint beamed. "You is right, sir. A wonder, indeed."

"A variable miracle," offered Sloth with a grand sweep of his hands.

"What?" said the man.

Slint pushed Sloth aside. "Show him no mind, sir. Words does come at him sideways betimes."

"Well, then," said the man, "what be the price, if price there be?"

"Ah," said Slint, "I sees you is a bargainer of the first order, so I shall not dicker and dacker with you. Ten sovereigns is the price."

The man laughed. These scamps in rags looked like they didn't have a farthing between them. "Why I'd have to have twice a thousand customers and more just to breaks even."

Slint shook his head vigorously. "But sir, think of the thousands and thousands who will pay. It be but a babe, which will grow as you grow rich over the years to come."

The man screwed up his face. "Here, let me have another look."

Sloth stepped forward and opened the sack. The beast of a babe bared its teeth and growled menacingly.

The man quickly peered in and then motioned for Sloth to close it. "A moment," he said. He turned and yelled at the van. "Enku, I's something you must see."

A small woman, white as the fallen snow and painted head to toe with bands of color jumped from the wagon and walked over to them, Slint and Sloth backing away.

"This be a witch!" screamed Sloth, grabbing Slint by the arm.

Slint tugged his hand away. "Quiet, I is negotiatin' here."

"She will not harm you," said the man. "Now, girl, take a look in the sack."

"Yes, Mr. Partly," said Enku.

Sloth was having none of it, handing the sack to Slint and backing away. "Here, you does it."

Slint grabbed the sack from him, stepped toward Enku, and opened it for her to peer inside.

A smile grew on Enku's face. "Why, it is just a babe," she cooed. "And the whitest white, like me."

"Will you care for it?" said Mr. Partly.

Enku looked delighted. "May I?"

"Here," said Mr. Partly. "Let her hold it a moment."

Slint offered Enku the sack, but instead of grasping it from the top, she cradled the sack and the writhing babe within in her arms, stroking it softly. The babe grew quiet and seemed to purr.

Mr. Partly drew a small leather pouch from his pocket and pulled out a single gold coin, which glistened in the sun. "A sovereign and no more," he said.

Slint and Sloth seemed transfixed.

"Two," said Slint after some moments.

Mr. Partly shook his head. "One," he said, holding the coin up. "Or none," he said, dropping the coin back into the pouch.

Slint looked like he'd lost a dear friend when the coin disappeared. "Well, then, how's about one and sixpence?"

Mr. Partly didn't hesitate. "One."

"One and fourpence? Surely you can spare a joey, if not a tanner."

"None." Mr. Partly took the sack back from an alarmed Enku as if to end the deal.

"One, then, one!" said Slint.

Mr. Partly handed the sack back to Enku. "One it is," he said, drawing the coin once more from the purse.

Slint grabbed the coin from him and raced away, Sloth in pursuit. Mr. Partly watched them go, shaking his head. "There be fools and there be fools, but we have seen the worst of them this day."

He turned to Enku. "Give it a care, dear, it looks snappish."

"It is but a wee child," she said, "and shall know love, whatever snap there be."

"In any case, we has made a fine deal this day. A fine, fine deal." He glanced back at the road. Slint and Sloth seemed to be doing a jig as they disappeared around the bend. "Fools, indeed." He turned and walked toward the wagon. *A cage*, he thought. *I shall need a cage. A strong cage. And chains.*

25

Port Famine, Strait of Magellan, June 4, 1836.

Zhao Yu saw them coming long before they spotted the cave, although he could not quite make out who they might be. Four men, all dressed in black, each carrying something long and silver gleaming in the sun. Swords? The emperor's assassins? It did not matter.

The time had come. He had expected it and was surprised only that he had not been dealt with long before this. He had failed his mission—the white dragon was dead. And he had begotten two monsters, half dragons, to complicate the mission. He knew they knew of one, but was confident the other's existence would remain unknown, whoever these assassins were, at least until it was too late for them to do anything about it. He would have his revenge.

Young Mr. Darwin was the key, of course. And thankfully, he had only seemed interested in the barnacles that encrusted the egg. He seemed to take all the talk of dragons as pure nonsense, which was fine. Yu had told him that whatever was in the egg was long dead, and Darwin had taken him at his word, not realizing that a living being was still in that egg, ready to hatch in just a matter of months.

Furthermore, he had no fears that the young man would report anything other than the story Yu had fed him.

"When you tell a big lie," he said to himself, lifting the pot from the fire and pouring himself a cup of tea, "it is always best to surround it with a sea of little truths."

He looked out the cave entrance. The men had spread out to assure he would never leave the cave alive. "And that lie will be the undoing of them all."

He dropped the powder into the tea and raised the cup to his lips. "Let us see what oblivion tastes like."

26

Home of John Stevens Henslow, Cambridge, England, October 10, 1836.

Henslow had never seen a man so crestfallen as the young man sitting opposite him at the table. Charles Darwin had come through the door a robust and cheerful young man not ten days removed from his arrival in Falmouth, but the news of the missing cask had quite stunned him.

"My letter will no doubt catch up to you in London," said Henslow, "but that does not change anything for the better. The cask is gone, perhaps forever. The search yielded nothing."

Darwin tried his best to form a rational sentence, but each time he started, he stammered, immediately stopping and looking blankly at his mentor and friend, now five years older, on the cusp of forty. Darwin was surprised to see how well he looked. In fact, he had fully expected to see a sick man, wasted away, his hair white, and his belly grown large. Instead, he saw the same man he had left, as handsome and ramrod straight as ever, the only sign of aging a slight graying at the temples. There was one remarkable difference, though. He now wore the white collar of a vicar. Darwin wondered how the man found time for those duties, let alone his professorship at Cambridge and his lifelong work in geology and botany.

Henslow tried to help. "But all is not lost, Charles. You found other examples of this barnacle, did you not?"

"Yes," said Darwin, "fully a dozen, teased from a conch shell, off the coast of Chile, but the egg, the *egg*, I have never seen the like."

"A loss to be sure, but just one among a thousand specimens that did make it back. Your catalog of achievements will not go unnoticed by the Geological Society, I assure you."

Darwin managed a thin smile. "I do so want to belong."

"I think I can say with some confidence that your membership shall come swiftly, and be well deserved."

Darwin nodded. "Thank you. Still, my notes, my journal— *gone*."

"But if I understand you correctly, the journal covers but a few days of your journey. Surely you can re-create it, at least in part."

Darwin knew he could, but thinking back on his days with the Chinaman, he wondered if he should. It was all so fantastical. And even more worrisome, now the whereabouts of his secret journal was unknown. If it suddenly appeared, the wild story it told could ruin him. People, his fellow scientists, and the Geological Society in particular, would laugh him off the stage.

"Yes," said Darwin. "Just a few days, a few *remarkable* days."

Henslow tried to distract him. "Tell me, what is so special about these barnacles of yours?"

Darwin beamed. "Oh, Henslow, when you see the new specimens, these *balanidae*, you will be astonished. They do not glue themselves to their host. They *drill* into them."

"Drill?"

"Yes, they burrow right in, through the toughest materials."

"God's wonders."

"Yes, if you will, and it is said that if they attach themselves to a living host, they change its very nature."

"Surely not," said Henslow. "I cannot see that as part of God's plan."

Darwin ignored the remark about God. He was no longer so sure that heaven had anything to do with how species behaved. "Yes, mere rumors, like their purported effect on Mocha Dick, but fascinating nonetheless, and worthy of further study, which is my intent."

"Mocha Dick? Really? Did you see him? I hear he is pure white."

"No, only heard the stories, Henslow."

"Well, that is interesting nonetheless." He paused, his thoughts transitioning from skeptical vicar to avid scientist. "But on the other hand, to study one, to *understand* one of these barnacles, will you not have to study *all* barnacles?"

"Yes, I have many specimens, but I will need more, collected from across the globe. I will need your help."

"Yes, of course, but that would take years, and you must deal with all the other specimens first and work on publishing your notes."

Darwin sighed at the ordeal to come. "Yes, 1,529 specimens by my count. But then I'll return to the barnacles. I am determined to have the answer."

He thought about the Chinaman and all he had said about barnacles—and *dragons*. He shuddered.

PART THREE

When I first saw him, it was as if I were looking in a mirror, so alike were we despite the obvious differences of sex and years. He stared at me, and I stared back at him, and for the first time, my transformation became more complete, unlocking a darkness in me I never dreamed was there: unfettered rage.

—Lily, *Interview with the Dragon* (excerpt)

27

Down House, Downe, June 4, 1844.

Emma Darwin set down the book she had been reading to Charles and glanced nervously at the clock. In a few moments, he would rise from the sofa and disappear back into his study. *Like clockwork*, she thought.

He had become a man of routine since they had settled at Down House just two years before, and she knew he would be loath to alter that routine for the trifling matter she was about to suggest. She had to be more circumspect.

"Charles," she began. "I have been thinking."

"W-what?" Charles stammered. For the past few minutes, he had been paying more attention to the gleeful sounds of Willy and Annie coming from the garden than to the soft, lilting voice of his wife. She had read *Pride and Prejudice* to him before, so he knew he could let his mind wander a bit, but he had clearly been found out.

"I said I was *thinking*."

"Oh? And what about, my dear?" She did not seem upset by his lapse in attention. *Curious.*

"It's been nearly nine months since Etty was born, and we have scarcely left Down House."

"Has it been that long? I've been so absorbed by the geology books."

Emma rolled her eyes. "Charles, you are always *absorbed*. What I am thinking is that perhaps we should spend a day or two in London. For once, I am not with child, and it would be good for both of us to take a break from work and routine *and* the children."

Charles smiled back at her. She was up to something, but he did not know what. If he had learned anything in the five years they had been married, it was that she could never carry off a deception of any kind. It was just not in her nature, and he loved that about her. In fact, he loved everything about her. Even now, in her mid-thirties, she was still a beautiful woman, with a burning intelligence, piercing hazel eyes, delicate features, and lovely brown hair, which she liked to part in the middle and curl along the sides of her head, as was the fashion. Most people called the side curls "spaniel curls," but Charles preferred to call them "hair falls" because they so resembled waterfalls, particularly when she moved her head. She was wonderful with the children and the servants, and equally important, she made a point of honoring the schedule he had laid out for himself. It was the only way he could get work done in the face of his near-constant stomach pains, gas, and nausea. Not even opium pills helped much.

Today, she was dressed in a brown, slope-shouldered morning dress, and she was saying something to him.

"Charles, did you hear me?"

"Of course," he said, and knew from the tilt of her head that she knew otherwise.

"As I was *saying*, we could run some errands—I really need to see a seamstress, and you could look at those new microscopes you have been so keen on—and then maybe we could take in an exhibition or an entertainment of some kind to round out the day."

Charles smiled. *An entertainment? So that is it.*

"And what sort of *entertainment* would that be?"

Emma sighed, knowing that she had been found out. "Well, I see in the *The Times* that there is to be a performance by that charming little man, General Tom Thumb, at the Royal Pavilion on 18 June."

Charles frowned. "The dwarf? Emma, you know travel is a problem for me, and sitting in a large hall — with my gas — would be terrible for everyone. Besides, I would much rather spend my evenings listening to a beautiful woman play her pianoforte to delight me."

Emma shook her head. "I do that every night, and not well. I need lessons. Oh, but we need something *different*, Charles. *Honestly.*"

Charles would not give in. "What of our backgammon games? You would miss them."

"Ha! I would miss beating you at backgammon, you mean. Charles, here is your chance to *not* lose for once."

"I do not mind that. I just so enjoy playing the game with you, the way your face lights up when you know you have me."

Emma stood and hovered over him. "So you would prefer losing again and again at backgammon to traveling with your wife to London for a *wonderful* day of shopping and amusement?"

Charles sighed and looked down at the floor. *I am not going to win this argument.*

28

The Royal Pavilion Theatre, White Chapel Road, Mile End, London, Tuesday Evening, June 18, 1844.

Charles sat with Emma in their box in the second tier and took in the opulence of the cavernous theatre, from the red velvet bunting that draped the boxes in each of the three tiers, to the massive curtain, also in red velvet, to the painted religious scenes on the dome above, saints and angels bearing witness to all below, to the four dome-high Corinthian columns that framed the stage, to the massive crystal chandelier hanging from the center of the dome, big as a railway car, casting a brilliant, sparkling light, making the dead white walls and gold trim dazzle, to the sights and smells of a writhing, cacophonous mass of more than three thousand spectators above and below them, waiting for the show to begin.

Emma had chosen their box well, one facing the very center of the stage. It had cost more, of course, but the privacy it afforded had put Charles at ease. If he had a problem with gas during the performance, only Emma would be affected, and she had long ago grown used to it.

Emma had never looked lovelier. He wondered whether this "entertainment" was just an excuse for her to wear her new gown, a stunning creation in royal blue, making him feel like a poor farmer as he sat there in his brown frock coat and matching vest. Spectators who looked into their box would no doubt think Emma was a wealthy single woman attended by her servant.

He had promised Emma that they would at least stay for the performance of General Tom Thumb, which came first on the playbill, but he would let how he felt dictate the rest of the evening. The effects of the opium pills were taking hold, so perhaps he would make it through the entire performance without the pain that usually plagued him.

The second feature of the night was the opening of a new play, a nautical drama called "Child of the Wave," which was described on the playbill as "the days of Queen Anne, received with shouts and laughter." He would be hard pressed to sit through that, but he knew that whenever they left would be too soon for Emma, who was clearly pixilated.

She reached over and touched his hand. "Is this not *wonderful!*"

He smiled back at her. "Yes, the theatre itself is a worthy entertainment. I have never seen such opulence."

"How do they make the chandelier so bright? It is like we are standing outside in the sun."

"It is a trick of the crystals, which are cut in such a way that—"

Emma interrupted him. "Never mind the science, Charles, here comes the master of ceremonies, or whatever he is called."

Three thousand souls, some slower than others, settled into their seats and grew ever quieter as the man crossed the stage, positioned himself in its center along the footlights, and bowed with a great flourish.

"Ladies and gentlemen, your kind attention, please."

He waited ten seconds, until the crowd grew still.

"Tonight's entertainments will begin shortly, and I promise you a full evening of wonder. You have seen the playbill and all that is to come, and yet, there is *more.*"

He let that sink in.

"From time to time, this theatre is presented with an act so extraordinary that we feel duty bound to push it to the forefront of our evening's performances. Such is the case tonight, when we present to you an act that will mystify and amaze."

He paused again, looking to each corner of the theatre, tier to tier. "Some of you may be frightened by what you are about to see, but I assure you, there is no reason for alarm. Your safety is always our utmost concern. Still, I would encourage the gentlemen in the audience to hold their lady's hand."

He paused and smiled broadly. "Just make sure she *is* your lady."

Everyone laughed. He nodded again and again, waiting for the laughter to subside.

"Now, without further ado, *"The Angel!"* He bowed and walked briskly off the stage as the massive curtain began to rise.

29

The Royal Pavilion Theatre, White Chapel Road, Mile End, London, Tuesday Evening, June 18, 1844.

The man continued shouting, "Curtain, curtain!" But the curtain did not move a centimeter.

Everyone in the audience was screaming and scrambling for the exits as the angel continued to transform, her angelic face now contorted into a long snout, razor sharp teeth flashing, drool spilling from her mouth, ears growing pointed, her dress splitting at the seams and falling away, revealing a scaly white body, a long, writhing white tail, and claws for feet. Her arms seemed to grow in length, dark talons emerging from her fingers.

She shook her wings and shrieked. The feathers fell away, revealing pale, membranous, bat-like wings that began to flap powerfully, lifting her off the ground to the length of her chains, which until that moment had been hidden behind white flower garlands.

One more shriek and a flap and the chains snapped. She flew into the air, circling the theatre, people in the upper tiers now ducking for cover or racing for the exits, tumbling over one another, screaming.

Darwin pushed Emma to the floor and covered her with his body. He couldn't see the beast, but he felt the wind she created with every circling of the theatre. Then he heard the sound of glass shattering and more screams coming from the people on the ground floor. He lifted himself up and peeked over the ledge. The beast was sitting atop the chandelier, making it rock back and forth, crystals raining down on the people below, its dark, flickering shadow cast eerily upon the dome. And then it saw him, sending a chill up his spine.

Darwin ducked back down. He could feel Emma trembling beneath him. "We will be all right. We will be all right." He heard the sound of flapping wings again, and then the scraping sound of claws digging into the ledge of their box.

He looked up. The beast was staring at him, not one meter away. He thought to drop back onto Emma. At least he could save her. But he was frozen with fear. He could see its face clearly now, and it was more dragon-like than human. And there was something else. Its head seemed to be encrusted in barnacles that pulsed with its every breath. *Barnacles!*

For whatever reason, the beast had grown quiet, sniffing at the air. Then it leaned in and sniffed at him briefly, the stench of its breath nearly causing him to faint. It seemed to smile at him, cocking its head as if it were trying to remember something. It leaned in again and sniffed at his head, smiling once more. *How in the devil could such a monster smile?*

And then, with one giant beat of its wings, it was gone, lifting up from the ledge and crashing through the roof of the theatre, plaster and lathe raining down on the few people who remained. And then all was quiet.

Darwin slumped to the floor next to Emma, who was attempting to get to her knees. "Charles, Charles!" she screamed.

He grabbed her and held her tight. "It's gone, Emma. It's gone."

"Oh, my God, Charles. What *was* that?"

"I do not know," he lied.

30

The Royal Pavilion Theatre, White Chapel Road, Mile End, London, Tuesday Evening, June 18, 1844.

Inspector Field tried his best to control the crowd, but they were in headlong retreat, pushing and shoving their way to the theatre doors. The best he could do was help the fallen back to their feet, so they wouldn't be trampled.

He glanced up at the beast, which was rocking back and forth on the chandelier, shrieking at the crowd below. For a brief second, he thought of joining the crowd, of getting out of this damnable theatre at once, but he was Inspector Field of the Detective, and by god, he would not leave his post.

He tried to focus on the four men he had been watching intently before the show began. Two were Chinaman, clearly, their shiny red clothing setting them apart, and seemed to be as pale as albinos, and they had now vanished entirely. Another, the albino man in black, had not moved an inch from his seat, and was staring up at the beast as if transfixed. And he was *laughing!*

Field quickly scanned the room for the other gentleman, the African in his strange robes, and found him in the center aisle, pushing his way through the crowd in the direction of the stage, where Field could see a diminutive woman, also an albino, staring up in delight and shouting something to the beast.

There was a sudden crash, and Field looked up just in time to avoid a falling timber from the roof, which now was open to the sky. The beast was gone.

He turned back to the stage. The albino woman was running across the stage, the African in pursuit. *My god, he has a sword!* Field raced after them, ignoring the man in black, who was now pushing his way through the crowd, headed for the doors of the theatre.

• • •

Barnum shouted at the stage hands to lower the curtain, but it was clear the curtain's ropes were tangled to the point of nonfunctioning.

The sound of snapping chains and her piercing shriek brought him back to the act, which had unraveled so quickly, he couldn't believe it. He stared in fear and wonder as she flew around the theatre. *What an act!*

Then he thought of General Tom Thumb. Where was he? Barnum looked around quickly, spotting the boy cowering behind a barrel in the wings.

"Tom!" he shouted, but the boy just stood there, unmoving.

Barnum raced across the stage, keeping a wary eye out for the beast, who now seemed to have perched on one of the boxes in an upper tier.

"Tom, come," he said, lifting the boy into his arms and racing back across the stage toward the little door that led to the alley and what Barnum hoped would be safety. Enku and that Abyssinian from the Rothschild's party seemed to have had the same idea, one disappearing after the other through the door.

"Wait," Barnum shouted, but they were gone, and nowhere to be seen once Barnum and Tom made it through the door themselves.

He put Tom down, took out a handkerchief, and wiped his brow.

"Damn," he said.

Tom nodded. "A fine mess."

A shriek forced them to look up. The girl was flying away.

"Come," said Barnum, "we must find Inspector Field and Mr. Partly and give chase!"

"Chase?" said Tom. "Are you crazy?"

Barnum managed a nervous chuckle. "I must be, I must be, but I *must* have her!"

* * *

Enku watched in wonder as the performance unfolded. She knew from the start that something was different. Lily was transforming so quickly, so completely, that Enku stood there in the wings, near breathless. It was as if the little girl she had raised had been replaced by a writhing, shrieking beast of incredible power.

She couldn't help laughing and clapping her hands with delight. This was Lily's chance! No one could stop her now!

"Go," she shouted up at Lily. "Go!"

Lily seemed not to hear her, so Enku started walking toward the front of the stage to try again. Then she saw the Abyssinian and his drawn sword, and stopped in her tracks. He was obviously headed toward her, and the look in his eyes was unmistakable. He was after her.

All the things that Enku's mother had told her, the stories of killing and mutilation, came rushing into her head. She turned and raced for the door to the alley, and once through, ran for her life, not stopping until the sound of her pursuer had faded to nothing.

She leaned against a wall, in a dark spot, far away from the nearest gaslight, and gasped for breath. Lily was free now, and so was she, although she didn't like her chances. Suddenly, a voice came out of the darkness, and a haggard man's face appeared in front of hers, lit by the light of a single match. He was dressed in rags and wrapped in a blanket. A street beggar, no doubt.

"Be you a ghost?" said the man, eyes growing wide.

"Aye," said Enku, thinking fast. "I've comes for your soul!"

The man dropped the match and raced away, leaving his blanket behind. Enku picked it up and wrapped it around her, forming a hooded shroud.

I must find a hole for the night, she thought. *But me Lily is free!*

• • •

The man in black knew what he was watching, even who he was watching, but if he had learned one thing during his time in England, it was self-control, not that this wouldn't be a test of the highest order.

He glanced to his left. The burly man leaning up against the wall in the far aisle was still watching him, a guard of some kind, a policeman perhaps, one of those new so-called detectives who gallivanted about the city in regular clothes, causing no end of pain to decent pickers and smashers.

He tried his best to ignore the man as the curtain completed its rise and nervous laughter broke out in the gallery. The girl was taller than he had imagined, but it was almost like he was looking into a mirror, her features were so like his, though smoother, smaller. She was clearly nervous, looking about in all directions, her body trembling.

He started rocking back and forth, hoping to attract her attention. When it was clear that he had, he removed his dark glasses and locked on her eyes, which widened noticeably. She began to transform.

The man pushed down everything in his being that screamed for him to transform along with her, just so he could watch, and learn. The ridiculous angel "wings" they had made for her exploded in a burst of feathers and her own wings, larger than he expected, and more powerful, flew open with the force of a sail catching wind. Her face began to change as she tugged at her chains, which he knew could not withstand the power she was unfurling. When they snapped and she flew into the air, he had to laugh at her owner's misunderstanding of her strength. She would be a formidable opponent, sister or no, but he knew he was stronger.

After poising on the ledge of one of the boxes, she suddenly flew straight up, breaking through the wooden roof of the theatre with preternatural ease. Perhaps he had misjudged her, and perhaps she does not know her own strength.

He raced for the theatre doors to see which direction she was headed.

• • •

Biniam Sahle quietly drew his sword and started making his way through the panicked crowd toward the albino man in black. The man was not the primary target, but Sahle knew the girl, now transformed, was out of reach and far too dangerous to approach, at least for now.

The man was probably stronger than the girl, but Sahle was adept with his sword and knew he could make quick work of him, especially since the man was just standing there, laughing, completely distracted.

He pushed on through the crowd, and then he saw her, an albino woman, an Abyssinian, no doubt, and a far more desirable target. The head and hands of albino women had much magic, and his father would be very pleased to add them to his collection, which had to keep growing to assure his emperorship and good fortune.

And now he could see that the woman had seen him, and was fleeing across the stage toward a small door. He picked up the pace and leaped onto the stage, the woman disappearing through the door.

By the time he got outside, he could see her at the end of the alley, running for her life as she turned the corner. He raced after her in the darkness, catching sight of her only when she was revealed beneath a gaslight. And then she would be in the darkness again. He ran as fast as he could, his legs burning, but the gap between them began to open, and finally, she was gone.

He came to an abrupt stop and stood there for some minutes, bent over at the waist to catch his breath. She was headed deeper into the East End, where even an elephant could disappear in its many dens, public houses, and dark holes.

He turned and headed back for the theatre. Perhaps the albino man was still there.

• • •

She could see the people in the gallery before they saw her, the curtain rising slowly, just as Barnum had instructed. She tried to calm herself, but she knew she was trembling. *Just get through it,* she thought. *There will be a chicken, there will be a chicken.*

She glanced to her right and left, finally catching sight of Enku standing in the wings. She was nodding and smiling at her. She seemed to be mouthing, "You can do this."

And then the laughter began, the crowd catching sight of her and reacting in a way that she did not expect. *Why are they laughing? Did Mr. Barnum plan this, too?*

She tried to block it out as Mr. Partly began his speech, which had the thankful effect of quieting the crowd somewhat, although some people continued to laugh and titter. Mr. Partly continued on, now raising his voice as a way to hush the crowd. His speech seemed to be working. The crowd was now quiet, rapt on his every word as he reached the cue for her to transform.

She scanned the crowd, eager to take in their reactions and to end any thoughts they might have that laughter was the right response to what she was about to do.

And then she saw him, a large man in black rocking back and forth in the center of the gallery, his hair and skin as white as hers. She watched as he slowly removed his dark glasses and stared directly at her. *He is me!* she thought, studying his face.

A chill came over her and then a deep heat like she had never felt before. Everything about her transformation was magnified, and she couldn't seem to control it. She felt stronger than she had ever felt before. And it was *intoxicating*.

She snapped open her wings and shrieked at the crowd, the chains snapping from her new-found power. The sensation of flight scared her at first, but only for a moment. Then she was circling the theatre, scattering the crowd. She landed on the chandelier to shriek at them again, these people who thought to laugh at her. They were like little mice.

A smell caught her attention, something from deep in her memory, a scent of long ago. She took flight again and landed on the ledge of a nearby box, where the smell was stronger. She peered down at a balding man cowering in the box, and sniffed at him. The smell was him. *How do I know this man?* she thought.

She peered down at the crowd. People were pointing up at her now, and she could see a strangely dressed man with a sword. Soon there would be men with guns. She flew straight for the roof, which gave way around her.

The cool night air felt wonderful.

• • •

Mr. Partly was doing his best, so he was more than a little angry that some of the people in the front rows were laughing at him and Lily. He hoped that Lily, standing behind him, would not take the laughter to heart and vary from the script.

He raised his voice. "Behold, then, a very angel from Heaven itself, come to Earth to delight and amaze."

He knew that Lily would now be unfurling her wings, and he noted a change in the faces of the crowd. Mirth had been replaced by wonder and whispered asides. Some seemed as frightened as they had hoped. A few were already trying to make their way to the aisles.

He paused to let them drink her in, then continued. "But why, ladies and gentlemen, why is she here with us now on Earth? Has she no heavenly duties? Could it be that she is a *fallen* angel, out of grace with our Lord?"

Partly could hear the loud clink and snap of the chains behind him. *That's not right.*

He pressed on, even as the crowd began to rise from their seats and scatter. "Or is she an angel from hell itself!"

His words were lost in her shriek, which shook him to his core. He had never heard her shriek like that. He turned and saw her lifting into the air, fully transformed and more powerful than he had ever seen her. She turned toward him and shrieked again.

He stood stock still, frozen to the stage, piss running down his leg.

31

Saint Giles, London, 11:00 P.M., Tuesday, June 18, 1844.

Enku trembled with fear as she made her way deeper into the maze of dark streets and alleys, her blanket now soaked through by a light but steady rain. She had no idea where she was going, but she followed the blurry light of the gaslights anyway, moving slowly while in darkness and quickly as she came upon the expanse of light from the next gaslight.

Passersby paid her no mind, though some stopped and looked back at her if they caught a glimpse of her pale face. Most just kept going, prompted on by the rain.

Enku suddenly stopped. There was a young girl standing in the light of the next gaslight, just a hundred paces away. She was pale, like Enku, and held out her hands as if to beg. She did not seem to be generating much business, given the way people arced around her and picked up their pace, despite her pleas.

Enku moved slowly toward the light. The girl could see her now, and startled, perhaps thinking her competition.

Enku raised a hand to calm her. "I am just passing," she said.

The girl looked her up and down, squinting to make sure she was seeing what she was seeing. "Am I wrong or do you be pale?"

Enku nodded.

The girl looked around warily. "Here now, be you alone? On these streets?"

Enku nodded again.

"Never saw you before. Are you begging, or on the run?"

"Running," said Enku, stepping closer. She could see the girl's face clearly now, a face that had once been heavily rouged to cover up her pale skin, but that now was a mess of red rivulets caused by the rain, making her look fearsome.

The girl looked up at the rain. "Not a good night for the likes of us. Come along, dearie, we cans gives you a spot for the night."

"Thank you," said Enku as the girl grabbed her by the hand and began tugging her down a dark alley.

"Keep up," she said. "We best be quick."

Enku picked up her pace, trying to keep up with the girl, who was now moving in a trot. The deeper they went into the night, the more their noses were accosted by a stew of sickening smells from heaps of filth and the slimy contents of bedpans emptied from high windows.

Enku held her breath and raced on as the bells in Saint Giles Church struck eleven.

32

Aftermath, The Royal Pavilion Theatre, White Chapel Road, Mile End, London, 11:30 P.M., Tuesday, June 18, 1844.

Inspector Field gathered his men in the gallery of the now empty theatre and told them to stand by while he talked with the gentlemen on stage, who were engaged in a shouting match over damages.

"Look what you has done!" shouted Crawford, the theatre owner, flailing his arms. "*Damages*, sir, damages beyond toll!"

"Nonsense, Crawford," said Barnum, cool as he could be. "A theatre owner must provide for risk, which I say was part and parcel included in your rental fee."

"Bollocks to that," shouted Mr. Partly, coming between them. "I's lost me acts! Me dragon girl and me white witch. *Fled!* Who's to pay for that, I ask you?"

Inspector Field strode across the stage, stepping carefully over fallen timbers and scattered playbills. The air was white with plaster dust, thick as many a fog he had seen, except for a patch of air near the chandelier, where a steady rain was falling through the gaping hole left by Lily, and pooling on the gallery floor. The absence of plaster dust there made it look like a column to heaven itself.

His forefinger was already wagging in the air, choosing a victim for his words.

"I shall tell you what you need and want," he said, his finger twirling to indicate he was directing his remarks to both Mr. Partly and Mr. Barnum.

"But first," he said, turning in a circle, arms raised to take in the devastation, "first we must address the topic of damages, as Mr. Crawford here rightly attests."

"Thank you, sir," said Crawford.

Field drew his finger back toward his own chest, then extended it, and waggled it at Crawford. "I think the thanks will be coming from Mr. Barnum here, sir, for as you know, I am a man of the law and have seen many a case of willful and not so willful damages."

"But all is clear," said Crawford. "Who could not say this, this *destruction*, be anything but willful?"

"Ah," said Field, wagging his deadly finger next to his nose. "Here be the truth of it. And let me make it point by point, so it be clear to you, clear to all."

Crawford crossed his arms and began rocking on his heels. "Go on, then."

"Thank you, sir, you are a patient man. I can see that clearly. Now, as to the first point, which is the act itself. Did you know that this act contained a risk? Perhaps a quite substantial risk?"

Crawford shook his head. "No, I assuredly did not."

"Not, sir? Not? Why did you not know that this girl or whatever she be—I have not seen the like—would be tethered in chains?"

Crawford nodded reluctantly, "Yes, but—"

"There be no buts, sir. Chains means danger where I comes from. Chains mean risk, real risk, and a full *panoply* of expectations. Do you not agree?"

"Well," said Crawford, befuddled, "well."

"Well, nothing," said Field, turning now to face Mr. Barnum, who had been smiling through it all. "Mr. Barnum, may I ask you a question?"

"Of course."

"Excellent. Well, then, Mr. Barnum, did you expect the destruction we see here before us?"

"No, of course not."

Field turned to Mr. Crawford. "Of course not," he said with a wag of his finger toward the ceiling.

He turned back to Barnum. "And tell me now, Mr. Barnum, did you not provide for said risk by means of chains to hold her firm?"

"I did, *we* did," said Barnum, giving a nod to Mr. Partly.

"Because?" said Field. Barnum wasn't sure how to answer.

"Because," Field continued, "because you had no *intent* to do harm. Is that not correct?"

Barnum beamed. "Why, yes, sir. No intent whatsoever."

Field turned back to Mr. Crawford, jabbing him in the chest with his fat finger as he made each point. "Now, Mr. Crawford, here's the truth of it, if you will. There being a general understanding of risk, *plus* a real attempt to mitigate that risk, *plus* an absence of intent on the part of Mr. Partly and Mr. Barnum, then there be no crime as such. There be only destruction and attendant costs, which if my vast experience serves, any court would find must be shared equally."

Barnum gasped. "What? Surely the theatre owner must absorb the costs as a factor in his rental fee."

"No," shouted Crawford. "No, sir!"

Field shook his head and tapped the dreaded finger to his nose. "No, Mr. Barnum, it is as I have said. Further, it is as I would *testify*, being a witness to the destruction itself."

Crawford seemed to be relieved, but Barnum was clearly unhappy. Even half these costs would set him back. He'd have to double Tom's performances, even increase the fees.

"I sees you is not happy, Mr. Barnum," said Field, "but let us now turn to the question at hand, and that be how do we find and deal with the creature who did these damages?"

"And me girl Enku," said Partly. "She be missing also."

Field nodded.

"I do not know which direction *she* went," said Barnum, "but I did see the girl flying toward the east."

"Ah," said Field, tapping his nose. "The East End I knows, and the East Enders knows me. I have transported more than a few of them to New South Wales. There be not a den or dark hole that will hide them."

"Good," said Barnum. "Let us conduct our search at first light."

"Nay, nay," said Field. "The peoples scatter with the sun. We must find them tonight."

Barnum nodded, reluctantly. The whole experience had been quite draining. "As you wish, sir."

Field smiled slyly. "There be a fee, of course, for the services of yours truly and his men."

Barnum rolled his eyes. "A fee?"

"Why, yes sir. A thing—or things—of value have gone missing. Surely, there be a fee for the search, perhaps even a reward for the finding."

Barnum nodded. He was resigned to it. He simply must have this new act, whatever the price may be. Within limits, of course. "And what fee and reward did you have in mind?"

"My men each get a pound for tonight's search, and I get ten pound. And when we find them, for we surely will, a reward of fifty pounds for each of them."

Barnum rolled his eyes as Mr. Partly's went buggy. "Fifty pounds!" they shouted simultaneously.

"Why, indeed yes," said Field, finger skyward.

Partly was shaking his head vigorously. "Me Enku is not worth more than a farthing, and I cannot affords no fifty pounds for the girl."

"If I may," said Barnum. "I shall provide the fees and the rewards for both."

Partly sighed with relief.

"On a condition, though, Mr. Partly."

Partly was wary. "And what be that?"

"On condition that you turn them both over to me."

"What?" said Partly, incredulous. "You would rob me?"

"Not at all, sir. When we find them, Mr. Field here shall receive his fees and rewards, and you shall receive a like amount for the transfer of these acts to me."

Partly seemed not to believe him. "A hundred pounds, *for them?*"

Barnum nodded. "A fair price, I think."

Partly beamed. "I do accept your offer."

"Well, then," said Inspector Field, "if your hagglin' be over, we must to it. We be losing darkness."

They moved for the theatre doors, Field adding one over-the-shoulder remark as they walked into the night. "And would someone please explain to me what I has seen this night, whether beast or practiced illusion?"

33

Saint Giles, London, 11:30 P.M., Tuesday, June 18, 1844.

They moved deeper into the darkness, through empty streets and alleys, each one filthier than the last, the bells of Saint Giles Church near lost in the sound of the pouring rain.

The girl suddenly stopped and pushed Enku against a wall, hushing her. "Be still. See there, those men?"

Enku looked across the dark street. Two shabbily dressed men, one sporting a slightly bent top hat, were having a smoke under the eaves of a ramshackle house that seemed to be leaning against the next one.

"That be Rat's Castle," whispered the girl. "Bad men. Thieves, and smashers, and pickers. We need to go back a ways, an alley I know, and go 'round."

"No," whispered Enku. "Look."

The two men were going inside, leaving the path clear.

The girl smiled. "Come, then."

They raced quickly and silently past Rat's Castle, then slowed two blocks later, when they came to Oxford Street.

"Here we be," said the girl, pointing at a manor house surrounded by a low brick wall. "A castle on the outside, but a flophouse within. Still, you cans have a sleep. Keep close to me and say nothin' till we's settled in with me family."

The girl put an arm around Enku and escorted her through the courtyard and the massive manor door, which squeaked loudly on its hinges. Enku gasped when she saw how many people were stretched out in a tangle upon the floor: men, women, children, mostly naked and reeking of sweat, and piss, and wet wool.

"Irish," whispered the girl, her only word of explanation. "Come, down here." She moved Enku toward a flight of stairs. If darkness could be darker than pitch, the basement was an exemplar. Enku was afraid to move for fear of tripping over the bodies she sensed were there.

The girl lit a match and soon three candles brightened the small room. "Not much," said the girl, "but choosers won't be beggars, and we calls it home."

Four pairs of eyes peered up at her, and Enku gasped. They were Abyssinians, and equally surprised to see her.

The girl held a hand to her chest. "I be Ibsituu, but you cans calls me Ibby, or Ib. This is my father, Neguse Zewedo, my mother Saba Tamrat, and my little brothers, Hassan and Etefu.

"Enku," said Enku, smiling and taking them in.

The man was tall and gaunt, more bone than flesh, unlike his wife, who was short and as plump as an orange, and clearly with child. The boys were scrawny, with eyes as big and as golden as sovereigns.

"Too many candles," said the father, scolding Ibby, who immediately snuffed out all but one, making everyone look more like flickering wraiths than people.

"I see that you are like our Ibby," said the mother. "How did you come to be here, and why is your hair so strange?"

Enku touched her hair reflexively. "Oh," she said. "It is part of my costume. They calls me Walla-Walla, the White Witch of Wongo-Bongo."

The woman's laugh was almost a cackle. "These Englishmens!"

Enku smiled at her. "Mr. Partly says it makes me look what he calls *exotic*."

"That be a new word, but I thinks I parse it rightly," said Ibby with a chuckle. "Your hair be strange, like a big ball of frightened wool."

"And why are you here?" repeated the mother with a look of concern.

"Running," said Enku.

The father looked alarmed and gave Ibby a withering look. "And you brought her *here*?"

Ibby shrugged. "She be lost, da'."

The mother pushed herself to her feet with great effort, gave her belly a soothing rub, and elbowed her husband aside.

"Do not worry, Enku. You cans sleeps here for the night, but *only* this night. Now, if you be on the run, best change your look. We have clothes that should fit, and some colored paste to darken you, but first your hair."

The mother nodded to Ibby. "Best get the razor, girl."

34

Saint Giles, London, 12:30 A.M., Wednesday, June 19, 1844.

As the clock of Saint Giles Church struck half twelve, Barnum and Partly followed behind Inspector Field, Detective Sergeant Rogers, and half a dozen constables through the rain-slickened streets. Rogers, looking as formidable as Field in his greatcoat, was leading the way, his lantern, his "flaming eye" in these dark streets, pointing the way.

They had already searched five lodging houses, with nothing to show for that smelly task, but Field was still moving swiftly, always sure that the next lodging would be the one.

"Close up, men," Field shouted over his shoulder. "Keep together, gentlemen; we are going *this* way!"

Now they were moving down yet another dark street, and it was clear from the way people avoided them that Field was a man to stay clear of, a man who could spot your guilt whatever it might be. Even crowds standing under the gaslights seemed to melt away before him. "Hook it," someone in the crowd would say, and the rest would scatter like rats. Oh, they knew their Inspector Field.

"Here we is, gentlemen," Field said, approaching the door of a house that seemed to tilt at an angle. "This be Rat's Castle. Stay close, and say nothing, for your safety depends on it. Do so and all will be well. They knows me, and I knows them."

He didn't so much as slow down, but proceeded into the establishment, his own lantern, what he called his "Bull's Eye" held in front of him, casting a yellow, dancing light on the men and women of sallow cheeks and brutal eyes huddled on the floor within, the smell of their vermin-laced clothing and bodies as formidable a weapon as a brace of pistols.

"Where be the Earl of Warwick?" asked Field, producing a truncheon from his pocket. "Come, my lad, I want you!"

Someone laughed in the darkness, and Field moved his beam to spot him. "Ah, there you be. Come forward, and take off that hat. An *earl* should know to uncover when greeting a gentleman."

A small man, bare to the waist and top hat in hand, stepped into the light and bowed. "Greetings, Inspector Field, and welcome to Rat's Castle, home of the best of the best."

Field snorted. "Best of the worst, you mean."

"I do indeed, sir. Thank you for the correction."

"Well, then," said Field. "I ain't here for any of you tonight. I be lookin' for two girls."

The earl laughed. "Why, sir, most of us be lookin' for two girls!" His minions in the darkness cackled with glee.

Field moved his fat finger through the air and jabbed the earl in the chest. "Enough, sir!"

Everyone assembled grew quiet. "One is full grown, about forty, an albino with hair as big as a bush; the other is about ten and likewise as fair and pale as snow." He thought to mention her wings, but thought better of it.

"We knows a few albinos, sir, beggars all," said the earl, "but none lodge here. They be bad luck, you knows."

"Wait," said a voice in the darkness.

"Who be that?" said Field.

A tall, gray, and soldierly looking old man stepped into the light.

"Ah," said Field. "You be Mr. Stalker if I have not missed my guess."

"The very one, sir," said Stalker.

Field laid his fat forefinger to his nose. "I knows you. You lived servant to a duke once?"

The man nodded.

"And what is it you do now? A begging-letter writer, I think."

"Oh, no sir," said Stalker. "Not me, no, I pick up work here and again, from place to place, on account of me delicate health." More laughter in the darkness.

"Very well, to your point?" Field leaned toward the man, hoping to receive an answer.

"Oh, right. Well, me and the earl here, we was havin' ourselves a smoke not an hour ago—I remembers the bells of Saint Giles was a strikin' half eleven—and I spies two albinos, much as you describe, cowering in the darkness. It be rainin' then, so I thought they were just tryin' their best to stay out of it, but—"

Field interrupted. "Where did they go?"

"I don't know, sir. We finished our smokes and went back in while they was still there next to the house across the way."

Field sighed. They could be anywhere.

"But that's easy to guess, sir," Stalker continued. "I knows one of them."

"What?"

"Yes, sir, an albino girl named Ibby, a right fine beggar. We calls her Ibby the Abby."

"Abby?"

"You know, sir, an Abyssinian."

Field turned and smiled back at Barnum and Partly before raising his forefinger and twirling it in front of Stalker's nose. "And where might we find this Ibby the Abby?"

35

Saint Giles, London, 1:00 A.M., Wednesday, June 19, 1844.

He moved through the darkness, following the scent of the woman as best he could, most of it cleansed from the sky by the rain, which had now thankfully ended. He had tried in vain to follow the girl, at least until the rain came, making it impossible. He knew she was long gone, perhaps even out of the city, but he could tell the girl had a deep connection to the woman who had been chased across the stage by that strangely dressed man. The color of the man had reminded him of the Fuegians he had once known, though their manner of dress was quite different. If he could find the woman, she might be able to lead him to the girl. With some persuasion, of course.

The sound of footsteps forced him into the shadows, behind a low brick wall that served to separate a grander home from the chock-a-block of now dilapidated homes, lodgings, and public houses that had been built right up to the manor's walls and seemingly left there to decay, leaving the manor house sitting there like a jewel in a dung heap.

There were maybe ten of them, including six uniformed constables. Two others, the ones with the lanterns, in plain clothes, were probably of that new breed called detectives. Caught in the middle and trying to keep up were two more men.

He recognized one as the emcee of the abortive show. The other was clearly a gentleman, but his clothes seemed foreign. Perhaps an American.

They seemed to be in a hurry and quickly made their way through the manor's gates and into the house. The clock on Saint Giles Church's steeple chimed one.

36

The Old Manor House, Oxford Street, London, 1:00 A.M., Wednesday, June 19, 1844.

Inspector Field didn't so much as knock as burst into the manor, its heavy doors shrieking, prompting a few screams in the darkness, which his lantern revealed was a gaggle of men, women, and children lying tangled half naked on the floor of an otherwise empty room, not a single stick of furniture in evidence. As grand as the outside of the manor house had been, this room, no doubt once a grand drawing room, was no more than a piss hole of foul people and their considerable assembled smells. *A fart wouldn't live here.*

"Who be in charge here?" Field said, knowing the answer and moving his light from face to face, most turning away and trying their best to resume what sleep was left for them. Even thieves had to sleep.

"Who be in charge? I said." Louder now, more demanding.

"Here," said a voice in the darkness, "as you well know."

Field moved the light in the direction of the gruff voice, revealing a haggard little man, bald as a knob, with a distended belly quite apart from his otherwise thin frame. Field recognized him at once.

"Why, if it isn't Blackey, Blackey of London Bridge, who has stood there these five and twenty years, skin awash and spotted in paints to fake disease."

If a man can look both sheepish and proud at the same time, Blackey had come as close as any. "The very same, sir, though now I spends me days more here than there. The duties of command, you see."

Field snorted. "Oh, and what a fine command," he said, holding his lantern high to take in the vile breadth and depth of it. "Looks all the worse for your command, sir, since Bailey's untimely death."

Blackey seemed not to take offense. "May he rest in one piece," he said in forced solemnity. He pulled a clay pipe from his back pocket and lit it, taking his time, drawing heavy on it until it glowed red. "Now, Mr. Field, I knows you is a busy man and does not come to my manor house for no reason. Please state your business, so my crew can go backs to the Land of Nod."

Field stepped forward and buried his fat finger in Blackey's chest, pushing him back against the wall. "We are *searching* for a woman and a girl, and *this* be the house where they are said to reside."

"There be many a woman and girl here, sir, from the basement to the eaves. Takes your picks and go."

Field released his forefinger, allowing the man to take a puff from his pipe. "I thank you for your hospitality, but we are looking for one *particular* woman and one *particular* child."

Blackey took the pipe from his mouth, but held it in front of his face, swirling it in the air as he spoke. "If we have your particulars, you are free to take them, jail them, transport them to New South Wales for all we cares."

"You should know one," said Field. "An albino girl by the name of Ibby the Abby."

Blackey brightened. "We knows her, sir, though some here calls her Ib the Ab, and others Lady Snow. A fine young lady, a beggar without peer. Lives in the basement with her family, Abbies all, though only she be a red-eyed whitey."

Field moved his lamp around the room, finally spotting the door to the basement. "We shall have a look, sir." Field turned toward the others. "Follow me and stay close. Now!"

They moved to the door and quickly descended the stairs, the room below dark and silent.

37

Outside the Old Manor House, Oxford Street, London, 1:20 A.M., Wednesday, June 19, 1844.

Biniam Sahle, envoy and son of Sahle Dengal, emperor of Abyssinia, crouched in the alley, away from the one bright gaslight on Oxford Street and peered across the way to where the albino man sat upon a wall that ringed a large manor house.

He had followed the man from the Royal Pavilion, hoping that he would lead him to the flying albino beast or the albino woman. And if that didn't work, perhaps Biniam could find just the right moment to ambush him, his tribe's preferred and long-practiced method of battle.

But now, looking at the size and bulk of the man—he was *huge* and clearly powerful—Biniam was not sure that his sword would be enough, even if he took the man by surprise, which might be impossible given the man's inherent wariness. He had never seen a man so alert.

Biniam moved deeper into the darkness of the alley. He could still see the man clearly, but he knew the man could not see him. He knew from experience that albinos could not see well, particularly at night. He just had to be still and silent, and wait for the man to make his move.

The door to the manor house swung open and two men with lanterns moved slowly down its steps, across the courtyard, and out the gate, followed by a half-dozen or more men, some in uniform. They paused briefly in the street, the sound of heated words filling the night until the bells of Saint Giles announced half one, which signaled the end of the argument and their swift march away from the manor house, headed west down Oxford Street.

The man waited until they had moved well away before he began to follow them, moving along the darkest side of the street to avoid the notice of a constable who had apparently been left behind. This development gave Biniam Sahle pause. *Why leave a man behind? To watch? Watch what? To Guard? Guard what?*

He thought to stay, but then decided to follow the man. He had lost two albinos this night. He would not lose another.

38

Basement of the Old Manor House, Oxford Street, London, 1:20 A.M., Wednesday, June 19, 1844.

Field slapped a hand against the wall as they reached the bottom of the staircase, the people in the darkness still silent. *They should be startled, even screaming,* thought Field. *But they are not. Something's amiss.*

"Awake!" shouted Field, and the denizens of the deep began to unfold their arms and raise themselves from the floor.

Field shown his light on them: a man, a woman, a young girl, and two small boys, all Abyssinians. He moved the light back to the girl, her eyes glowing red in the light. "If I am not mistaken, you be Ibby the Abby."

The girl nodded. "Ibsituu Neguse, if you please."

"No need for formal airs, girl. Let's stick with Ibby."

"As you wish, Mr. Field."

Field could not help smiling. "Ah, I sees you knows me."

"Who does not, Mr. Field? These be your streets."

"Indeed, they are," said Field, setting down his lantern. "Now, *Ibby*, I have but one question for you, and we shall all be gone."

"As many questions as you like, sir."

"Good, good, I like the way you yield to authority. It is very becoming for a girl such as yourself."

The girl shrugged. "Your question?"

"Where is the woman, the albino woman?"

Ibby looked puzzled. "Woman? What woman would that be, sir?"

"Now, now, Ibby, it do you no good to lie. You has been seen, you see, by none other than a fine gentleman at Rat's Castle."

Ibby snorted. "There be no gentlemen there, sir. And he be mistaken, whoever he be."

"Did you not pass by the castle this very night, escorting an albino woman?"

Ibby started to shake her head, then brightened, as if she had remembered something. "Oh, *Oh*, you means *her*, that woman. Yes, a small woman with a poof of white hair, wrapped in a blanket and looking like a drowned rat. She come upon me in the rain, asking for directions to the West End."

Field squinted at her, not sure of her story, but the woman was clearly not here, so maybe the girl's story held water.

"Where in the West End?"

"Why, I asked the same thing, sir, but she just wanted to be pointed west."

"So you—"

"Pointed her west, sir, and off she went, fast as a pickpocket with a new watch."

Field picked up his lantern and scanned the room again. Nothing and no one.

"Gentlemen," he said. "We search this house top to bottom, basement to eaves. If she be here, we shall find her. If not, we goes west."

39

Outside the Old Manor House, Oxford Street, London, 1:30 A.M., Wednesday, June 19, 1844.

Barnum could no longer contain himself. Staying silent so long, particularly forced silence, was completely outside his character. So as they stepped through the gate, Barnum pounced on Field.

"We will never find them!" he shouted.

Field stopped in his tracks and began poking Barnum in the chest, each word louder than the next, ratcheted up to near a bellow. "We shall find her, sir. Anger is not what we needs."

"But we have accomplished *nothing!*"

"Nothing? Nothing, sir? We shall have her, if not tonight, then tomorrow!"

"But how? We must have been in a dozen dozen vile dens this night, and nothing to show for it!"

The bells of Saint Giles Church chimed half one.

"Half one, sir, just half one, we still has time, so let us move as quickly as we can."

Barnum sighed, resigned to continuing but wishing he was home in bed, listening to the General's soft snore. "Very well, let's to it."

Field turned to one of the constables, whispered in his ear, then turned back to the group. "Now, gentlemen, we move back to Saint Giles Station, where we shall partake of coffee and cakes and unfold the rest of this night's plan. Jeffries will stand post here. I have me doubts about the girl's story, so best to keep a watch."

They moved west, picking up the pace, shadows of men disappearing in the wake of their bright lanterns.

40

Saint Giles Station, 2:15 A.M., Wednesday, June 19, 1844.

By the time the group reached the station house, their number had dwindled to three: Field, Barnum, and Partly. All the other officers had been sent one by one in different directions, each to a different police station to widen the net, each with but one instruction: round up every albino in London and bring them to Saint Giles Station post haste.

Barnum was relieved to get off his feet and delighted by the ongoing show coming from the small cells that lined the back wall: a drunken hag, raving mad and threatening to write the queen *this very day* to gain her release; a silent woman with a child to her breast, arrested for begging; the woman's husband in a smock-frock, shaking his head and pacing back and forth with an overflowing basket of wilted watercress; a young boy, a pickpocket surely, rolling a coin back and forth across his knuckles, giggling all the while; and a meek pauper man, moaning loudly, head in hand, the effects of liquor shining red in his eyes and pooled on the floor. The air was redolent of ale and sweat and piss and vomit.

The three of them were seated around a large table to the left of a bench where a portly sergeant sat twirling his moustache, his eyes fixed on the door, waiting for the next criminal to process.

Barnum put down his cup. "Your coffee is as bad as your tea is good."

"We tries," said Field, waving a lemon cake he held daintily in his large hand, a surrogate for his deadly forefinger, now busy holding the cake.

"Or maybe it's just this foul air," said Barnum. "I do not know whether I am tasting coffee or —"

"Exactly," said Field, holding his cake high.

"I have surely had worse," offered Partly.

Field started to set down the cake on the bare table, thought better of it, and then placed it on a stack of papers in the center of the table. "Now that we have had our cakes and coffees, however good or bad they were, let us to the task at hand."

"Indeed," said Barnum. "What exactly is this plan of yours?"

Field pushed back his chair and paced in front of them, waving his finger in circles as he spoke, as if it was the crank for the pump of his words. "We have alerted every district and ward as to the subjects of our search, even the Thames Police, who will also search for bodies among the piles and posts and sluices."

"Bodies?" said Barnum, alarmed.

"Albinos are both feared and hated, Mr. Barnum. If they made the mistake of walking along that dark river, they could have met men even darker than the ones you seen this night."

Partly shuddered. "You don't think?"

Field paused in his pacing long enough to lay a hand on Partly's shoulder. "We musts be brave and think the best."

"So what now?" said Barnum.

"The hardest thing, sir," said Field. "We waits."

"Waits?" said Partly. "Is that all?"

As tired as he was, Barnum agreed with Partly. They needed to be out there, searching. Field could see he was about to object, and held up his controlling finger.

"My men and the men they recruit and the men *they* recruit will bring our desired subjects here. I am sure of it."

Barnum slapped his hand on the table, his face red with anger. "Well, why did we not do this from the very start, instead of traipsing aimlessly through these foul streets?"

Field frowned back at him. "Aimless, sir? Why, not in the least. My intent was to proceed as quickly as possible to the most likely places of hiding."

"Well, that did not work, did it?"

"No, sir, it did not." His words came out slowly, measured, as if he was about to explode. "But," he said, jabbing his finger at Barnum, "it be what it be."

Barnum rolled his eyes and slumped back in his chair. There was no use in further engaging this obstinate man in civil argument. "All right, then. We follow your so-called *plan*."

"I agrees," said Partly, who knew not to argue with Inspector Field.

"Then we *waits*," said Field, sitting back down and drumming his fingers on the table.

The drunken woman began screaming again, this time claiming that her husband was a captain in the royal dragoons, who would *this night* confront Queen Victoria herself to remedy this maltreatment and unseemly incarceration.

Field sighed and turned to the sergeant. "Sergeant Baker, would you kindly release that woman and all the others. We will be needing those cells. Soon, I think."

The sergeant nodded and eased himself off the high stool, wincing from the pain of rampant hemorrhoids.

"No better, Sergeant Baker?"

Baker shook his head silently and grabbed the ring of keys for the cells.

"My wife, Mrs. Fields, has a cream, Sergeant, which will work wonders on those piles."

"I would much appreciate it, sir." The sergeant moved to the cells with clear discomfort and began releasing his prisoners, the screaming woman first. In less than a minute, the cells were empty, their contents spilled back into the maw of night.

"More coffee, gentlemen?" said Field.

41

Outside Saint Giles Station, 2:30 A.M., Wednesday, June 19, 1844.

The man in black watched the group grow smaller one by one, constables peeling off in different directions until finally there were only three men to follow, and them not for long, all disappearing into a building marked with a shiny brass plate announcing "Saint Giles Station."

He took a position across from the station, away from the gaslight, and gazed down the street, looking for the strangely clothed man with the sword. He wasn't sure who the man was, or from where, but he had enough experience to know that the man meant him harm.

He had to smile at that. The man was laughable. His puny sword was laughable. *Let him come*, he thought, and his wish was quickly answered, the man appearing as if on command, moving slowly toward him, staying close to the wall of the building. Just a few more steps and he would be within reach.

Suddenly, the doors to the station swung open with a bang and a motley crew of men and women shuffled down the stairs and scurried away in all directions, like insects released from a bottle.

He watched as they disappeared into the darkness, then turned to check the progress of the strange man, who was now inexplicably striding boldly up the steps and into Saint Giles Station. *What was he up to?*

Whatever it was, the man in black had had enough for one night, at least in these streets. He knew the girl would appear when she was compelled to appear, that she would have no choice in the matter, and he also knew he was stronger than she was. He would let her come to him, whether that be in a day or a year or longer.

He threw back his cloak, unfurled his large gray wings, and lifted into the air. The bells of Saint Giles Church chimed half two.

42

Saint Giles Station, 2:30 A.M., Wednesday, June 19, 1844.

Field leapt to his feet when he saw the Abyssinian come through the door.

"Sergeant," he shouted, "seize that man!"

The sergeant, grimacing in pain, did his best to clamor off his high stool, but the best he could manage was a slow descent.

Biniam Sahle took advantage of the delay. "Hold, sir, you may not arrest me. I am the envoy of Emperor Sahle Dengel, may he rule forever, and am not subject to your laws."

Inspector Field closed the gap between them and began poking Biniam in the chest with his fat finger. "I shall tell you what you are, sir. Envoy or no, you is the man who this night brandished a sword in the Royal Pavilion and chased after an albino woman, obviously meaning her harm."

Biniam started to object, but Field poked him again, harder. "Further, you meant to do harm to at least one of two subjects we are seeking this night, for their safety and the safety of all."

Biniam was shaking his head vigorously. "I drew my sword for my own protection and did nothing more than flee, just as everyone else did."

By now, the sergeant had worked his way behind Biniam, finally grabbing him and forcing his arms behind his back.

"No!" screamed Biniam, but the sergeant persisted, shoving him toward a cell. Field took advantage, deftly plucking Biniam's sword from its scabbard and tossing it onto the table, startling Barnum and Partly.

"Cell one," said Field. The sergeant continued shoving until Biniam was safely behind bars.

"You shall pay for this!" said Biniam through the bars. "The queen will be displeased."

Field chuckled. "You are not the first person this night to know the queen. Now, if you want out, I suggest you best start with the truth."

Barnum was on his feet. "Inspector Field, he is who he says he is. I met him some nights ago at the Rothschild's."

Field nodded and twirled his finger in the air. "He is who he is? Well, then, that is half the truth. We still must examine the issue of the sword and its use in pursuing Mr. Partly's albino woman. Am I the only one who saw his intent?"

"I saw him running with the sword, but I was behind them and could not see his face," said Barnum.

"And you, Mr. Partly?" said Field. "Did you see him?"

"No, sir," he said sheepishly, brushing at his still damp trousers. "I was, well, focused on the girl, you see."

Field began pacing silently in front of the cell, finger to nose, trying to parse out the situation. Finally, he stopped and turned back to Biniam.

"Let us say, sir, that all you say is true. That you are an envoy I have no doubt. Mr. Barnum's word, you see. But your *intent*, that is still in question, though we have no proof—*as yet*, that is. But even if there was no intent to harm the woman, there is still one very curious question, sir."

Biniam looked puzzled. "Question?"

"Indeed," said Field. He motioned toward Barnum and Partly. "The three of us have spent countless hours searching for the girl and the woman you chased across the stage, with no results—*as yet*. So the question is how you come to be at this particular station, at this precise hour?"

Biniam smiled. "I can answer that, sir. I came here for safety, yours and mine."

Field seemed dubious. "Safety? And just how is that, if I may be so bold to ask?"

"As you say, I did draw my sword. I also chased after the woman, but not to harm her, sir. She seemed to know where she was going, and I sought to follow her to safety."

"Safety again," said Field.

"Yes, and once outside, I stopped. The woman continued running, and just before she turned a corner, I saw a man in black, a big hulk of a man, racing after her."

"Was he albino?"

"Yes, I believe he was. Anyway, he looked menacing, so I thought to follow them, to perhaps come to the aid of the woman, if necessary."

"And did you?" said Field.

Biniam shook his head. "No, she was too fast for the both of us, and when the man stopped in his tracks, so did I, making sure he could not see me."

"And then?" said Field.

"And then I followed him for some while—he seemed determined to find her—and then you and Mr. Barnum and some others suddenly appeared, marching down Oxford Street with obvious purpose. The man hid in the shadows, as did I, and then he began to follow you. I stayed close behind, wondering what he was up to."

"And?"

"And he led me here. He's outside now, across the street, lurking in the shadows. I think he is after the woman and thinks you will lead him to her."

Field's mouth dropped open, his lips flapping silently for some seconds before he found the words. "Sergeant, with me!"

He turned and raced for the doors, throwing them open with a bang and racing into the street, the sergeant moving along as best he could behind him.

43

A field outside London, 4:30 A.M., Wednesday, June 19, 1844.

Lily sat under a tree, her wings held over her head to shield herself from the last drops of an overnight rain, which now dripped from the leaves above. Her flight from the theatre had been exhilarating at first. She had tested her wings with turns and loops and dives, scaring more than a few people below. But then the rains had come and flying became an ordeal that quickly tired her.

She was weary, and naked, and hungry, and shivering, and wasn't sure how to proceed. She had seen a man the very image of her, a man who had stirred something within her, a danger, a fear, a rage, and a *longing* she could not explain. She felt she was supposed to *do* something, but what? And then there was the man in the theatre box. She knew him somehow. His smell was so familiar, a smell suggesting her very beginning, her birth. It was all overwhelming.

Enku! she thought. *Poor Enku, where are you?*

She tried to calm herself with the certainty that Enku must be safe within Mr. Partly's wagon. Lily would go back for her, so they could be together again. Partly was afraid of her now, she could see that clearly back at the theatre. He would not put up a fight, she was sure.

But first she wanted to find the man in the balcony. If she went back to the theatre, perhaps she could pick up his scent. She looked up at the sky, which was brightening to greet the new day. The sound of a nearby rooster startled her. She turned in its direction, where she could see a small farm house.

She tucked in her wings and strode across the slick grass. "Chickens!"

44

Saint Giles Station, London, 7:00 A.M., Wednesday, June 19, 1844.

The night had been nothing less than a parade of albinos of every size, shape, sex, and ethnicity. But no Enku and no Lily. And Biniam Sahle had been released, disappearing as quickly as he had arrived.

Mr. Partly, who had been mostly silent during the previous night's searches through the lodging houses, public houses, dens, and other dark holes in the East End, had become extremely animated and verbose as the albinos came streaming in, one by one, each accompanied by a constable, sometimes alone, but often with irate family members trailing behind, demanding to know what was going on. The whole scene had given Mr. Partly a case of the giggles, because here before him now was the answer — perhaps many answers — to his loss of Enku and Lily.

As each albino was identified as "not Enku" and "not Lily," Partly was on them, whispering in their ears or their parents ears about the delights and rewards of the show business. By the time the last albino left the station, he had recruited three for his show, including a young dwarf he planned to bill as a "mushroom-boy."

Barnum was as somber as Partly was giddy. They had lost the girl, and he was not confident that Mr. Field of the Detective was up to the job of finding her.

And now here was Partly, joining him at the table and chuckling to himself. "Oh, this be a fine morning," he said, pouring himself another cup of coffee. "I has three new acts. *Three!*"

Barnum frowned at him. "But we have lost Lily. Are you not concerned about that? And what of your Enku?"

Partly screwed up his face as if the sound of their names was like lemons. "Pah, I told you she were trouble, and Enku was getting too old. New blood's what I need, and new blood's what I have this fine morning."

"I saw your new blood," said Barnum. "They are not worth a farthing, the lot of them."

"What, did you not see the dwarf, then? That big head of his and the long white hair. I shall be calling him the *mushroom-boy*. All he needs is the right cut to his hair."

Barnum had to laugh at that. "Mushroom? Are you crazy?"

"Not at all," said Partly, adding a lump of sugar to his cup. "I am a showman what knows his stuff."

Barnum rapped his knuckles on the table. "A showman who has lost his *one true act*."

"I do not believe so," said Partly. "Besides, she ate too many chickens."

Barnum sighed heavily. "Go on, then. Go to your mushroom-boy. May he make you a wealthy man."

Partly slurped down the rest of his coffee, gave Mr. Barnum a quick nod, and left the station, leaving Barnum brooding at the table.

Mr. Field caught sight of him, and his mood, and joined him. "Quite a night, was it not?"

"Bah! We have *nothing* to show for it."

"Ah," said Field, placing his forefinger aside his nose. "We has clues."

"Clues? What clues?"

"Well, leads."

"Leads?"

"Well, we has at least eliminated every albino in London who is neither the girl nor the woman."

Barnum rolled his eyes. "And you see that as progress?"

"Why, surely, sir. We will find them now, find them quick."

Barnum pulled a small black book out of his pocket and flipped through its pages. "Here, I shall be leaving for Europe at the end of the month. Till then, I shall be arranging performances for the General, hopefully including Queen Victoria herself."

"I have no doubt you will, sir. The queen is said to like foreigners, and oddities."

"So, here is what I am trying to say. You have until the end of the month to find the girl—I do not much care about the woman—but at month's end, my offer of reward shall end."

"I understand you completely, sir, and shall redouble my efforts on your behalf. We shall find her."

The bells of Saint Giles chimed seven.

45

Barnum Residence, Grafton Street, West End, London, 8:30 A.M., Monday, June 24, 1844.

Barnum sipped at his third cup of coffee, a stack of newspapers spread out before him, some dailies, some weeklies, and each with a different story to tell about the "strange goings-on" at the Royal Pavilion Theatre.

The first story, brief and sensational, had appeared on Wednesday in the *Evening Star*: "Flying Beast Attacks!" screamed out from the front page, followed by just two paragraphs that would have made any reader run indoors and stay there. Large dailies like *The Times*, *The Star*, and *The Examiner* picked up the story on Thursday morning, adding more details, including brief comments by the theatre owner, Mr. Crawford. Thursday's papers included breathless eyewitness accounts, and by Friday, the stories had moved from the front page to page three, most rehashing what they had already printed, but with additional details on the damage to the theatre or "new theories" about whether the monster was real or just an intricate piece of Barnum stagecraft that went wrong. By Saturday, even some of the small papers like *Cleave's Penny Gazette*, *Age and Argus*, and the *London Mercury* had picked up the story, most copying the larger papers almost word for word, although their stories were overshadowed by a fully illustrated story in the *Illustrated London News*, which showed Lily three times her size, with teeth as long as knives. The most complete, almost rational story, including interviews with Crawford, Barnum, Partly, and Field, appeared on page seven of *The Sunday Times*. In it, Lily was portrayed as a freak with vestigial wings, an aberration of birth. Whether she flew or had been hoisted into the air by thin, sturdy wires was left to the imagination and conjecture. Source of the damage to the theatre was also subject to conjecture, some building engineers claiming that the roof itself was faulty, an "event waiting to happen."

And now, on Monday morning, the story had all but disappeared, with *The Times* offering only a paragraph, printed deeper in the paper.

"It is like the Tower of Babel," said Barnum, tossing *The Times* aside.

"And none on the mark," said the General, his voice a bit difficult to understand.

"Do not talk with your mouth full. You did that last evening, *in front of the queen*."

"She was right amused, I think."

Barnum chuckled. "She was, she was, and very generous in the bargain. We shall go first class through Europe, I can tell you that."

"And when shall that be?"

"At the end of the month. I have already booked us passage to France.

"Quelle merveille, monsieur!" said the General, affecting his best Napoleon.

Barnum had to chuckle. "Merveilleux en effet!"

They both seemed pleased, and settled back to the task at hand, toast with marmalade.

"So," said the General between bites. "Any word from our Mr. Field?"

Barnum frowned. "Not so much as a peep. We have no doubt seen the last of him and our would-be act, more's the pity."

The General smiled broadly.

"What are you smiling about?" said Barnum.

"I am glad she is gone."

"Jealous, are we?"

"Pas du tout, monsieur, not at all."

"What then?"

"Elle est trop dangereuse."

"Dangerous, yes, but what a wonderful act she would be. And to your benefit, sir. She would draw even bigger crowds for you, and even larger purses. Why, your clothes would be made of gold, sir."

The General smiled, then quickly frowned. "Non, elle me mangerait dans son ensemble!"

Barnum laughed. "Eat you whole? Well, now, I would certainly have something to say about *that*."

The General began giggling uncontrollably, slapping his little hand down on the table.

"What is this paroxysm of glee about?" said Barnum, himself now swept up in the giggling.

The General forced himself to remain calm long enough to blurt out, "I would not hear you from her stomach!"

46

Whitehall Place, London, 5:30 A.M., Tuesday, July 1, 1844.

Inspector Field sat on a bench in the dim pre-dawn light, elbows on knees, head in hands, pondering the situation. To him, there was no better place for reflection and contemplation than this courtyard: the Great Scotland Yard. Policemen in the brightly lit house behind him were busy with the details of various crimes, but here, here he could escape it all and sort out whatever knot needed untying. And a knot it was.

Every effort to find the girl and the woman had been for naught. The immediate search had failed. The rounding up of albinos had failed. Subsequent searches high and low had yielded nothing.

He had gone back to the theatre several times, hoping through conversations with the theatre owner to come up with some clue that would drive him forward. He had taken up one such clue, interviewing Baroness Rothschild in her gilt world to get her views on what had transpired, but all she could offer in any detail was a description of a "wonderful" blue gown worn by an "elegant" woman in the next box, the same box the girl had chosen to land on. She had an eye for fashion, but not for beasts. All Field had come away with was a new definition of "opulent."

He had also checked in with Mr. Partly, to see if the man could offer any information about the girl that would help him track her down. Partly seemed disinterested at best, so taken was he by his new acts, particularly his mushroom-boy.

"The boy is a natural, Mr. Field. A right ringer."

Field had frowned at that. "I am certainly happy for you sir, and for your dear mushroom-boy, but I am here, you see, on another matter, your so-called dragon-girl and her companion."

Partly had just shrugged. "I tolds you all I know." He then went on a rant of all he had told Field previously: how she looked; how she behaved; the manner of her transformations; her annoying habits; and what she liked and did not like—all within the ticking of two minutes.

Field had left knowing nothing new, leaving him sitting on this bench in the Great Scotland Yard, watching the sun rise, complete with the sound of a far-off rooster announcing the new day, a day Field knew would find Mr. Barnum on the shores of France. No girl, no reward.

And then something Mr. Partly had said came scratching and clucking into his head. "Chickens!" he shouted, jumping to his feet. "By god, she likes chickens!"

He turned and raced into the house, grabbing the first person he saw, Detective Sergeant Moreland, by the arm. "Bill, gather the men. We need every newspaper from every town and village from here to Liverpool, for the last week. And make ready for a long day and night. We shall have many a pub and farmhouse to visit in the countryside. Oh, and carriages, enough for a dozen men."

Moreland nodded quickly at each command and then marched into a nearby drawing room that had been converted into a desk-filled office, now occupied by twenty of Scotland Yard's finest. "Gentlemen, your attention, please," he shouted.

47

Down House, Downe, England, Tuesday morning, July 1, 1844.

Since the incident at the Royal Pavilion, Charles and Emma had barely left the house. He had cancelled his daily walks through the garden, afraid of what might come from the skies. His symptoms—intense stomach pain, nausea, flatulence—had come crashing down on him with a vengeance, making work in his study near impossible. Not even double doses of opium pills had tempered his difficulties. If anything, the pills had left him drowsy and disoriented.

Emma had been especially shaken. As she read to him now, he could hear it in her voice and the way the pages shook as she fumbled to turn the page. She was reading Jane Austen again, his favorite, but the words seemed to make no sense, as if the sentences were falling apart, words floating away.

His mind was elsewhere, tortured by the memories that had come rushing back: the man in the cave, the barnacle-encrusted egg, his secret journal, their loss in transit to England, his fruitless search for them. And now that the monster had revealed itself, he knew that his secret journal must also be in England. He didn't know whether he could survive the embarrassment it would cause him if someone discovered it and published it for all the world to see.

It would ruin him. The theory that he had been setting down as a draft would never find a publisher. Or if it did, it would be discounted as the work of a lunatic.

If he could just ride this out — surely someone would find and kill the monster — he and his theory would be fine. A dead monster would back up everything he had said in the journal.

But what if the monster found him first?

He could not shake the image of the beast leaning in and smelling him at the theatre. It seemed to know who he was.

"The smell of the documents," he said.

"What, dear?"

He didn't realize he had said the words out loud. "Sorry, Emma, I was just lost in thought for a moment."

"You have not heard a word, have you?"

He shook his head. "No, I am afraid I have not."

She slapped the book closed, lips trembling, and began to cry.

"Oh, Emma," he said, rising from the sofa to console her. "Please forgive my lack of attention. It is these damnable pills, I think."

Emma sniffled. "It is not that, Charles."

"The Royal Pavilion?"

She nodded and burst into tears.

He rubbed her back gently. "You will be fine, I will be fine."

"Oh, truly? And *when* will that be? I am shaken to my very bones!"

He ran his hand softly across her head. "It will pass, and soon."

Her trembling continued. *And what if it does not pass*, he thought. *What if the monster comes for me?*

He would have to finish the draft of his manuscript, then write a letter to Emma, with instructions on what to do with the manuscript in the event of his death. But he would wait a few days, until she had calmed down.

"Come," he said. "I think a walk in the garden with the children will be good for the both of us." *And monster be damned!*

48

Whitehall Place, London, 1:00 P.M., Tuesday, July 1, 1844.

It had taken all morning to gather the major London newspapers, and still more were coming in from the countryside, smaller newspapers that focused solely on news of importance to farmers and landowners, from grain and livestock prices, to farming methods, to local gossip.

Field's team was looking for one thing: any stories related to disappearing chickens or other livestock. Any such story was quickly clipped from the paper and pinned to the wall for later examination. Every policeman's hands, and many a scratched nose, were now black from the ink.

Their efforts had yielded plenty to look into; that was certain. The wall was streaming with smudged clippings, most decrying an apparent surge in mischievous foxes, some suggesting the work of mythical beings, from fairies and trolls, to the many variations of demonic black dogs that filled the nightmares of farmers: Gwylligi, Black Shucks, Freybugs, Guytrashes, Padfoots, and Cu Siths. Several articles mentioned a crow the size of a man, who apparently preferred sheep. Those were set aside in favor of more than a score of articles about missing or mutilated chickens.

Inspector Field paced in front of the wall, quickly realizing that some sorting was needed.

He turned to Constable Pickens, who was the lead clipper. "Pickens, you have done remarkably well, and yet." His voice trailed off.

"Sir?"

"Well, we have a wall of articles, but they are all mixed together. Let's move all the articles about chickens to that wall over there, sorting them first by location and second by time—when the events took place, you see."

Pickens huffed and sighed at the work he knew would be required, then nodded. "Yes, sir."

"And I need that done within the hour."

Pickens eyes grew wide. "But—"

"Or the half hour."

"Yes, sir," said Pickens resignedly, turning to the men closest to him. "Bartly, Morgan, here!"

They began sorting, moving from wall to wall, the "chicken wall" slowly beginning to take shape. Field left them to it and went outside to his bench. He had thinking to do. Serious thinking.

49

Down House, Downe, Tuesday morning, July 1, 1844.

The walk in the garden had improved Emma's spirits and Darwin's, at least enough for them to return to their daily routine. They had slept soundly for the first time in days, and were now engaged in a breakfast discussion of child rearing as they watched their children's nurse, Brodie, chase Willy, age 5, and Annie, age 3, around the table, bouncing baby Etty, just ten months old, on her hip, the little girl giggling from the boisterous jostling. The whole room smelled of bacon, freshly baked bread, and raspberry jam.

To help cheer herself up, Emma had put on the new dress she had purchased during their day in London. It was a pale yellow, slope-shouldered dress, pleated at the waist, with puffed sleeves and accented by a bold pattern of red clover leaves. She looked wonderful, and he had told her so.

"There should be rules, Emma," he laughed. "Are we raising little savages?"

"Indeed, we are, Charles. And you will be happy for it. We want children who will think for themselves and not be mere lemmings to authority."

Charles glanced at his laughing children as they made another circuit of the table. "I think there is no fear of that, Emma."

He grabbed Annie as she ran past, and tickled her, Willy pulling up sharply. "Me, too!" he screamed.

Charles was about to grab Willy, too, when he noticed his manservant, Joseph Parslow, trying to get his attention. He let Annie go, and stood.

"Yes, Joseph, what is it? You look concerned."

"A young lady at the door, asking for you."

"For me?"

"Yes, sir. Barely ten years old, I would think, and dressed in rags. An albino, if I am not mistaken. Very fair and quite beautiful. I asked her to leave, but she would not. Says you know her."

Charles didn't hesitate. "I know no such person! You will have to be more firm. Send her away!" *It must be her! Come to kill me!*

Emma interrupted. "Charles, where are your manners?"

He bent down and whispered in her ear. "It may be her. *It.* From the Royal Pavilion."

"What?" she said, shaking her head impatiently and turning to Joseph. "Does this poor little girl have wings?"

Joseph seemed startled. "Why, no, madam."

"Sharp teeth?"

He shook his head. "No, a wonderful smile."

"See, Charles, you are being silly. More likely another hungry little girl. We have plenty. Let her in. We will prepare a basket of food for her."

"No," Charles said firmly. "I shall handle this."

He walked past Joseph and down the hall to the front door, where a young girl stood in the doorway, silhouetted by the morning sun.

She was wearing a brown linen dress too large for her small frame, and it was stained and tattered in the bargain. She did, indeed, look like any other poor waif you would pass along the road, except for her pale complexion and whitish blond hair, which was dirty and tousled and filled with leaves and small twigs, as if she had been sleeping on the ground.

But she was not just any poor waif. He recognized her angelic face immediately.

"Off with you!" he said as firmly as he could manage, but he knew his voice was quavering nervously. "There is nothing here for the likes of you."

The girl stood her ground and smiled up at him. "You need not fear me, Charles Darwin. I mean you no harm."

Charles stopped three paces from the door. *She knows my name!*

"Why have you come here?"

The girl sniffed the air. "I have a memory of you, from before."

"Before?"

"My birth. I remember only a dark place and the smell of wet grass — and *you*."

Charles grew more alarmed and insistent. "See here, now, you really must go!"

The girl nodded. "I will leave, and never return, but first I would like you to answer two questions."

Charles looked behind him. Emma was peering around the corner, as were Willy and Annie. All were nodding.

He turned back to the girl. "Then ask them, quickly, and be on your way."

The girl nodded and took a step inside the house. "*Who* am I?" she said. "*What* am I?"

Charles shuddered.

PART FOUR

He was nervous in those first days, our Mr. Darwin, for as much as he wanted to learn all about me, he was also very frightened of me. It took some time, many walks 'round the garden, many talks in his study over tea, for him to finally grow at ease with me. Then, though we became friends, his approach to me was more as a scientist. I was his riddle, his Gordian Knot, and more — I was the fly in the ointment to everything he believed and propounded about species. I sometimes thought he would have been very pleased if he could have crafted a well-reasoned sentence that would cause me to evaporate before his eyes.

— Lily, *Interview with the Dragon* (excerpt)

50

Down House, Downe, Tuesday morning, July 1, 1844.

Lily sat back in the high-backed leather chair in Mr. Darwin's study, slurping indelicately from a cup of tea, now grown cold, and quietly watching the dust motes swirl around him as he tried to explain, in words and gestures, who she was and, more important, *what* she was.

The sunlight was pouring into the room from two open windows to her left, making Mr. Darwin, seated at his desk opposite her, appear ruddier than he actually was. He was a tall man and fairly thin, with a pronounced stoop to his shoulders and the beginnings of a paunch under his brown waistcoat. His hair was dark brown and obviously receding, creating a vast pate above his bushy eyebrows, which seemed to dance as he spoke. He had the bright eyes of a man who laughed a lot, although when he fixed his gray-blue eyes on her, she had the feeling that he was looking into her very soul. The room itself, with its full wall of books and a table and desk cluttered with manuscripts and biological specimens, suggested a man of the highest intelligence.

She did not know quite what to make of his story — it was so fantastical — but she knew in her heart that it was no more fantastical than her ability to transform herself into a dragon-like creature, and therefore must be true.

He had seemed nervous at first, stuttering a bit and clearly a little frightened, which was understandable given their first meeting, when she had transformed to her dragon state during a theatre performance gone terribly wrong. The crowd at the Royal Pavilion had made her nervous and agitated, so she had transformed fully, as never before, breaking her chains and flying around the theatre, creating a headlong panic among the theatre goers. It was then that she had smelled him, his scent all too familiar, a scent that had led her to his door to find out how she came to be.

Once into the story, however, Darwin had calmed down considerably, even laughing from time to time, slapping his knees at how preposterous the story sounded. She had been hatched from an egg, he said, an egg he had shipped to England in a small cask that had been lost upon arrival, along with some letters and a small journal, which accounted for his scent being so prevalent at the time of her birth. Or so he surmised.

"But the story gets stranger still," he said, waving his hands in the air, the motes dancing. "Your father was a Chinaman named Zhao Yu, who like you, was afflicted with a condition that robbed him of all color, his skin pale, his hair white, his eyes, like yours, the lightest blue and seemingly red at times."

"And my mother?" she said, setting her tea cup aside. She liked the tea—a new experience for her—but the fine china felt strange on her lips, nothing like the tin water bowl provided by Mr. Partly, the man who called himself her master, a man she would thankfully never see again. She was free now, and intended to remain so, come what may. Still, she worried about Enku's fate.

"A native Fuegian," Darwin continued, "and by Yu's account, the most beautiful woman he had ever seen."

Darwin looked at the girl opposite him, herself a rare beauty, perhaps only ten years old or so. Her features were part Chinese and part Fuegian, giving her an almost Polynesian aspect. She was dressed in an ill-fitting linen dress, no doubt taken from a clothesline and now torn and tattered by days on the road, sleeping in fields and woodlands. She smelled of sweat and grass and urine. Her silvery white hair glowed in the morning light. *I will have to get Emma to bathe her*, he thought. *And perhaps some new clothes.*

He leaned back in his chair, giving his head a little shake. "But for you, it is more than just a father and a mother."

She raised an eyebrow. "Oh? How so?"

"Put simply, or at least as simply as I can, your father had the blood of a red dragon coursing through his veins. Your mother, in turn, had the blood of a white dragon coursing through hers, put there by Yu as a way to give her near immortality in much the same way that he had received it from the blood of the red dragon. He loved her very much, and wanted her to live forever with him."

"*Near* immortality?"

"Yes, they could be killed — and I suspect the same is true for you — but other than that, they neither aged beyond their twenty-first birthday nor fell victim to diseases of any kind. Or so Yu said."

"So they are both still alive?"

Darwin let out a big sigh, the motes swirling away from him. "Your father, almost certainly. Your mother, no. She died in childbirth."

"The egg."

"Yes, it was covered with sharp barnacles."

She reflexively touched the now smooth bumps at her hairline. "How could that be?"

"I do not know. According to your father, the egg of the white dragon he was charged with guarding had become encrusted with a unique barnacle during the voyage from China, a barnacle that bored through the shell and somehow infected the dragon within. And that dragon's blood, the blood he had given your mother, carried certain traits of that barnacle."

"The throbbing bumps I get on my head when I change?"

"I think so."

"They drive me crazy. I seem to lose all reason."

Darwin remembered all too well what she looked like and how aggressive she became when she transformed, and shuddered.

She picked up on his concern. "Do not worry, Mr. Darwin. I have nothing but kind thoughts about you."

He gave her a weak smile. "There is something else you should know."

"Yes?"

"Your mother gave birth to an egg—you—and a live child, your brother."

She blanched. "I think I saw him—at the theatre."

Darwin's eyes widened. He remembered the tall man in black. "You must be wary of him. According to your father, your brother—and you—are on a quest, a dangerous quest to find and kill a green dragon yet to be born. And that is just the beginning."

He paused, not sure whether he should tell her, but then decided he had to—her life depended on it. "More important, only one of you can survive."

She gave him a puzzled look. "Dragons? A Quest? And I am to kill my own brother? Or he is to kill me?"

Darwin pushed back from his desk, picked up the teapot that his Emma had left them, and walked over to Lily.

"Let me freshen your tea. It is a long, complicated story."

51

Whitehall Place, London, 5:40 P.M., Tuesday, July 1, 1844.

The sorting had taken far longer than expected, the task growing larger and larger as more newspapers were added to the mix. But finally, the chicken wall was complete and ready for Mr. Field's examination.

Pickens and his men had done a fine job, so Field had let the black-fingered men go home, with instructions to return by dawn the next day. By then, Field would have a plan and they would set off in carriages for the countryside.

The chicken reports broke down into six columns representing small towns southeast of London, each of which reported unusual chicken incidents on consecutive days: Chartwell, the town farthest away, on Wednesday, Westerham on Thursday, Hawley's Corner on Friday, Biggin Hill on Saturday, Laytham's Crossroad on Sunday, and Addington on Monday. The reports of missing and mutilated chickens were nearly identical.

He moved to a map Pickens had added to the wall, and followed her path with his forefinger. She was headed back toward central London, or so it seemed. She could be anywhere, but the direction seemed clear enough, the towns aligned in a northwesterly path from Crawley to Addington, all linked by the same road.

He noted the distances between the towns would be a good day's walk for a child her size. She was probably on foot then, reluctant to spread her wings, perhaps. He marked the distance and then drew a circle to determine what other towns were within walking distance.

The circle included South Croydon to the west, Leaves Green to the east, Farleigh to the south, and West Wickham—the most likely town—to the north. They would need to check out each of them—their farms, manors, and public houses—as well as all the roads that ran from those towns to central London.

Field tapped his finger against his nose. She would stay close to the roads but probably keep to the tree line, where she would be less likely to be detected. And then she would strike at farms along the way. *Chickens of opportunity*, he thought.

He smiled at the phrase. *Well, I do believe my Mr. Dickens would like that one.*

He and the young author, just thirty-two to Field's thirty-nine, had become friends through a chance meeting in the middle of the night some months ago. Dickens suffered from insomnia, and as Field learned, roamed the dark streets and alleys of London to pass the time, as well as to ruminate on his plots.

Field had made a point of timing his own patrols to cross paths with him, so they had spent many a night walking stride for stride with one another, the underbelly of London on full display for their examination.

Field also made a point of not overly praising the young man's work, although he could not resist telling him how much Mrs. Field had admired his recent work, *A Christmas Carol*. She had read it three times, and always cried with joy at the end.

Field sighed. She had also talked endlessly of Christmas and was already adding ever more decorations to their small home, even though it was still July. Every day there was a new garland or bow to greet him.

Field would have to tell Dickens about that, too, if he ever returned from Italy. He missed him, and knew he would have greatly appreciated Field's current adventure with the winged beast of the Royal Pavilion.

Field glanced at the map once more, then grabbed his hat and headed for his waiting carriage. What would it be tonight? A new garland or a Christmas goose served five months early?

52

Down House, Downe, 6:00 P.M., July 1, 1844.

Darwin had told Lily everything, even things he knew were too fantastical to possibly be true, like the "fact" that her father claimed to be hundreds of years old. Morning had worn on to evening, Lily asking questions and Darwin doing his best to answer them.

One thing was clear to Darwin: she was articulate and extremely intelligent, with a quick mind and an uncanny ability to jump obvious questions to reach more telling questions. She got to the heart of matters.

"It begins to make sense," she said. "My change at the theatre being so strong. It was his presence, as if just being near him triggered something from deep within. It was like a fire."

"Do you think it was a call to your quest?"

Lily shook her head. "No, I think it was more like *here I am, fear me*. But I could tell he was shocked and amazed at my transformation. It was *he* who was afraid."

As well he should be, thought Darwin.

Little Annie came bursting into the room, racing to Darwin and jumping into his arms. She was already the apple of her proud father's eye, a girl possessed of a spontaneous affection for whomever she met. "Mum says *dinner!* Come!"

Darwin gave her a hug and set her back down. "Annie, I would like to introduce you to Lily."

Annie beamed, walked over to Lily, and began stroking her hair. "Why are you so white?"

"Now, Annie," said Darwin. "Let us not be rude."

Lily grabbed Annie's hand and held it in hers. "I am not sure, Annie. Why are you so *pink?*"

"Pink?" Annie giggled, turning to her father. "Am I really pink?"

Darwin laughed. "Relatively speaking, Annie. Now, we should not anger your mother. I can tell from the smell that we are having a fine chicken tonight."

Lily beamed. "Chicken? I love chicken."

"Me, too!" squealed Annie.

Lily gave her a surprised look. "Do you change, too?"

"Change?" said Annie.

Darwin intervened. "Never mind that, let us to the table."

They left the study and walked down the hall to the dining room, which was aglow with candles and lamps. Emma, the governess, and the other children were already seated at the large table, set handsomely with their finest bone china, a wedding gift from Emma's father, the famous potter Josiah Wedgwood, dead now almost a year.

"Take your seats, everyone," said Emma. "Charles, please carve. The bird is getting cold."

Darwin motioned Lily into a chair opposite Emma, and then lifted Annie into a chair next to Lily.

"Well, then," he said, picking up a carving knife and fork. "Guests have first choice, Lily, so which do you prefer, light or dark?"

Lily looked down at the featherless, crispy brown bird, a puzzled look growing on her face. "I thought you said we were going to have chicken?"

"Yes," said Darwin, pointing the knife and fork at the cooked bird. "Here, before you. Does it not look *delicious?*"

Lily leaned in to get a closer look. "It looks dead."

Darwin chuckled. "Well, of course it is dead." And then it hit him. "Lily, were you expecting a *live* chicken?"

Lily nodded, beaming. "Yes, do you have one?"

Emma's mouth slowly dropped open as Annie began giggling. "Me, too!" said Annie. "Feathers and all!"

53

Outside the Old Manor House, Oxford Street, London, 9:00 A.M., Wednesday, July 2, 1844.

If there was one thing you could say about Constable Jeffries, it would be that he was persistent to a fault. They didn't call him "bulldog" for nothing. So, even after being relieved of his watch nearly two weeks prior, he continued to check in on the manor house, hoping to apprehend the albino woman. She could be his ticket to an appointment to the Detective.

He would lurk in the shadows at dawn and watch in almost disbelief at the steady stream of pickpockets, smashers, and beggars scurrying out of the manor's doors, some even running to their tasks and chosen spots around London. Later, after his normal duty was up, he would return to watch the same horde straggle back in, looking more haggard than they had in the morning, if that was even possible.

So it continued, day after day, until this morning, when he noticed something that had escaped him: a small woman in a dark cloak, easing her way out of a basement window and making her way through the overgrown shrubbery that surrounded the home. A flash of pale skin was all he needed to confirm his prey.

He stepped out of the shadows and followed her at a distance as she made her way down Oxford Street, heading toward Saint Giles Church. There were two ways to get to the church. You could walk straight down the road or take a faster route through an alley that served the church's cemetery. When she took the straightaway, Jeffries turned into the alley and raced to and through the cemetery, jumping over headstones as he zigzagged his way to the church itself, finally pressing himself up against the wall of the church and peeking around the corner.

She was coming toward him now, just steps away. The bells of Saint Giles chimed nine, loud and clear, startling him enough that he gave a little shout.

He looked around the corner. She was running.

54

Down House, Downe, 9:00 A.M., Wednesday, July 2, 1844.

Emma was beside herself, shaking with anger, and Darwin was having a hard time calming her down.

"I cannot *believe* you would suggest such a thing," she said, pacing in front of him.

"Now, Emma, hear me out."

"Hear you? I *have* heard you. You want me to bring a *beast* into our household. Forget the theatre. Did you not *see* what she *did* to that chicken?"

Darwin tried not to think of the way Lily had ripped the cooked chicken apart when she had learned there would be no live chicken. "Granted, she needs instruction on manners."

"Manners? She near ate it whole, then spat it out—right onto the table."

Darwin tried not to smile, but the one thought that came to mind was how Annie had laughed and clapped her hands at the sight.

"She prefers live chickens for now. We can work on that."

Emma stopped pacing, and hovered over him. "What is there to smile about? Is this funny to you?"

"No, of course not."

"She is *dangerous*, Charles. Those teeth!"

"Yes, she can be dangerous, but not towards us, I am sure of it. And as for her manners, well, it is all fixable. I mean, no one has taken the time to instruct her otherwise."

"And you would have *me* do that?"

Darwin shrugged. "Or Nurse Brodie. Lily is very smart. I am sure she would be a quick study — and she could be a great help to you and the children."

"The children, Charles, the *children?* Just think of the children, then. Would you like to see her rip them apart as well?"

Darwin sighed. "Emma, my dear, I have spent many hours with her. She would not harm any of us. She is lost in the world, with no place else to go."

"Take her back to the theatre. Find her owner."

Darwin shook his head. "You would see her in chains, treated like an animal?"

"Well, she *is* an animal."

"Emma, please sit. I have something *important* to tell you."

Emma sighed and sat down, exasperated.

"Well then, Emma, the *truth* is she is both human *and* animal, an impossibility made manifest, and I mean to discover by what means she walks among us now."

Emma slumped back in her chair. "Science again, your *natural philosophy?*"

Darwin brightened. "You remember the barnacles I told you about? They had a part in her creation, I am sure of it, but how?"

"And what if they did? Of what import is that?"

Darwin grew serious. "As you know, I have been working on a theory."

Emma nodded. "Yes, yes, that in species, favorable variations will tend to be preserved, and unfavorable ones to be destroyed."

He smiled back at her. "Yes, that is part of it. Two years ago, I expanded my thoughts to thirty-five pages. And now, even before Lily's sudden appearance, I have been steadily improving upon it. I dare say, it will exceed two hundred pages, perhaps much more, when I am done."

Emma gave him a puzzled look. "And how is this relevant?"

"Why, her very existence puts the entire theory in jeopardy."

"So?"

"So I have to see how she fits, if she fits at all, and revise my speculations accordingly."

"But Charles, you have already promised to publish your geological observations of South America. How will you find time for studying her and those barnacles of yours?"

Darwin shook his head. "I simply must, you see. It is all the same puzzle."

Both grew quiet, Emma finally breaking the silence.

"So you would place our safety at risk to study this girl, this *specimen*?"

Darwin rolled his eyes. "Are we back to that, then? Emma, I assure you, there is no risk. Give it a week. If you still feel endangered, I shall make alternative arrangements for her."

"A week?"

"Yes."

If Emma knew one thing, she knew science would win in the end, and so she put off her best judgment, and relented. "Very well, but just a week."

Darwin smiled. "That is all I ask."

"Go then, *shoo!* Go study your *specimen*."

She watched him go, a dance in his step. There just was no stopping him when it came to science. *A week*, she thought. *Can I even last a day?*

55

The Blue Lion, West Wickham, 6:00 P.M., Wednesday, July 2, 1844.

Six farms and four pubs later, Inspector Field had all but given up, the pint of ale before him of more interest than the search for the girl.

He had sent carriages in every direction, along every possible road to the farms and pubs mentioned in the myriad clippings from the chicken wall. His men had all returned here, to what Field called his "Field Headquarters," with nothing new to report. The girl had seemingly vanished.

There were stories aplenty, of course, of missing and mutilated chickens. One farmer reported "nothing left but feathers," another "not so much as a feather," and still another "just heads and feet." One thing all the stories had in common was how quietly it had been done, "without the usual ruckus of, say, a fox or a weasel."

Inspector Field surmised that the girl had simply walked up to the chicken, throttled it, and shoved it into her long-toothed maw. He shuddered, remembering her fearsome look as she flew around the theatre.

And now she was gone, out there somewhere, searching for her next chicken. The only fact that gave him respite was that she appeared to be holding close to London. Perhaps he would find her yet.

He sighed. *Of course there would be no reward, not now, with Barnum already in France.* Unless he caught her quick, and sent word to Barnum. That thought gave him at least some hope.

Someone tapped him on the shoulder. Field turned to see a ruddy, moon-faced man as short as he was wide, a long clay pipe dangling from the man's chapped lips. He smelled of manure.

"Yes?" said Field.

The man smiled and took the pipe out of his mouth, smoke curling around him, which he waved away with his meaty, callused hand. "I hears you is the head man."

Field nodded.

"Well, then, I seen what you seek, yesterday, at me farm."

"A young girl, one of the pale folk, about ten years old, perhaps with wings?"

The man looked puzzled. "Why, no. A young man, if you can call him that. More like half dragon. Tall and burly, dressed all in black. But yes, with wings—and a tail."

The man glanced over his shoulder at a group of men sitting hunched over a table, laughing. "They think I am right ready for Bedlam, but I knows what I sees."

A chill went up Field's spine. *The man from the theatre, the man who followed us through the East End?* "A man, you say?"

"Yes, a pale one for sure, with long silky white hair. Took one of me sheep and flew away with it, easy as you please."

The laughter grew louder, Field silencing them with his booming voice. "Yes, sir, that is *exactly* who we seek!"

As the laughing men sat stunned and slack-jawed, Field motioned the man toward the door. "Come, we will see your farm. Men, to me!"

56

Whitehall Place, London, 8:40 P.M., Wednesday, July 2, 1844.

The trip to the man's farm had yielded nothing more than boot prints in a muddy patch of field. Field had thanked the man, giving him directions for what he should do if he ever saw the man — or the girl — again.

And so they had returned to Whitehall, Field wanting nothing more than to dismiss his men and spend a few reflective moments on his bench in the courtyard of the Great Scotland Yard before taking leave himself to head home to Mrs. Field and her ever-growing Christmas displays.

But a beaming Constable Jeffries had put a quick end to Field's plans.

"Sir, we has her!"

Field's heart leapt. "Where, where is she?" he said, eyes going wide.

"In the lower cells, sir, and right ready for your inspection."

"Well done, Jeffries!"

Field and Jeffries moved quickly through the house and down the long flight of stairs to the basement, which had been converted into a guard's area with six heavily barred cells. When Field saw her, a heart that had once leapt, now sank.

"*Her?*" He glowered at Jeffries, who was taken aback by the look.

"Why, yes sir, the one we was lookin' for back at the old manor house. I caught her sneakin' out. It was quite a chase, and—"

Field cut him off. "Never mind, Jeffries. And I do apologize for my reaction. I was expecting the other one, the flying one."

"Yes sir, sorry sir."

"No need for that, you have done well, better than all the rest of us. We have spent a long day chasing our tails, whilst you have made a right fine catch."

"Thank you, sir."

"Now, run along home. I will stay a while to converse with the woman. Perhaps she can lead us to the other one."

"I would be happy to stay, sir."

Field recognized his ambitions and had long ago decided to recommend him for promotion to detective constable. He liked the man's doggedness above all else, and at well over six feet tall, he made for an imposing figure, a man who could loom over suspects and express his will over them. He was also square-jawed handsome, which would come in handy prying information from the ladies, from hags to princesses.

"Now, Jeffries," he said, poking his fat forefinger on the man's chest. "I knows what you wants, know that nothing would please you more than to be made a detective constable. And as I sees it, you are well on your way."

Jeffries smiled broadly.

"Even so, a detective must sleep."

Jeffries dropped the smile.

"Do not be discouraged. Let us talk more of this on the morrow. But now, if you do not mind. . ." Field motioned him to leave.

Jeffries nodded and turned for the stairs, a near cheek-breaking smile growing on his face once more.

Field waited for him to reach the first floor landing, then grabbed a chair and dragged it down the line of cells to Enku's cell. She stared out at him through the bars.

"Why so glum?" said Field, positioning his chair opposite her and sitting down.

She motioned with her hands to take in the limited expanse of the cell. "This."

Field smiled back at her. "Why, I hears you spend many an hour in a cage, at least if Mr. Partly is to be believed."

She nodded and looked away.

"Now, now, no need for a mood. We shall talk, you and I, and at the end, you will have a choice of your own choosing: walk free or return to Mr. Partly."

"You will not keep me?"

"No, of course not. All I seek is information on your young flying friend."

"I do not know where she is. If I did, I would be with her."

Field cocked his head to one side and tapped a finger beside his nose. "Indeed, I do believe that is true. But, yes, I do seek her, for Mr. Partly and Mr. Barnum have offered a fine reward for her return, a reward that you might share in should you supply me with information that might lead me to her." He didn't like to lie, but he often found that lies led to the truth, particularly if used properly and judiciously by Inspector Field of the Detective.

Enku crossed her arms. "I do not seek a reward, and hope you never find her. She is free, and that is something she has never tasted."

"Very well, but *your* freedom depends on answers to certain questions."

Enku frowned. "What sort of questions?"

"Why the easiest questions to answer, my dear. Here be an example. When did you first meet the young lady?"

Enku smiled, thinking back on that day. "It was ten years ago. Two men, wharf rats from Liverpool by their accents. They come upon our traveling show with a jiggly sack. Mr. Partly, he looked in first, then had me look in." She paused and chuckled to herself.

"Yes?" said Field. "And then?"

Enku giggled. "It were a baby, white as snow, like me, and in a terrible mood. But as soon as I picked her up, she quieted and almost cooed."

"Yes, how sweet, but what has happened twixt then and now?"

"At first, very little. She was a newborn baby, you see. My job was to care for her between my performances."

"As the White Witch of, um, *Whatever*."

"Wongo-Bongo, actually, but yes. And it was tiring. She were not no normal baby now, was she? I had to deal with more than just changing nappies."

Field nodded. *Oh, I bet you did.* "Tell me about these transformations, the way she changes."

"Well, sir, until the Royal Pavilion, I would have to say that her changes were mild and infrequent. If she were very hungry, say, she might extend her tail or flap her little wings in defiance or, in the worst cases, extend her snout and bare her teeth. But the Royal Pavilion was something else."

"Is she dangerous, do you think?"

Enku shook her head vigorously. "No, sir, she has a big heart. I have never seen her harm anyone, at least on purpose. I have me scars, of course, from when she was a wee one."

"Tell me about the Royal Pavilion. When I saw you on that stage, you seemed almost gleeful."

"Oh, yes sir. I kept telling her she was something more, that she was more powerful then she knew, and I was right."

"Indeed," said Field with a quick nod. "But tell me more. I have heard her *shriek*, but does she *speak*? Can she carry on a conversation?"

Enku beamed proudly. "Oh, yes sir. I taught her to speak and to read. She knows her letters and her maths, and she is accomplished at both. Dress her up like a right fine young lady, and you would never know she were different — *mostly*."

"Mostly?"

Enku nodded. "She do like her chickens, sir."

Field nodded back. "I have certainly seen the evidence of that this day. So, no cooked food?"

Enku frowned. "It were Mr. Partly's doing. He said he wanted her a bit wild, wanted to let people see her attack live chickens. Makes them afraid. Good for business, he said. And besides, she had a taste for it. Loves her chickens, she does."

"I see. So then, in your opinion, is she a freak — you know, a human with a terrible physical affliction — or is she something other, a monster?"

"Lily be no *monster*, sir," she snapped. "And she be no freak, neither. Bearded ladies are freaks. Same for the very tall and the very small. But she, she sir is something else, something *more*. I cannot tell you what exactly. All I knows is that I loves her."

"And would you say she loves you back?"

"I dearly hope so, sir." She put her head in her hands and began crying softly.

"Rest now," said Field, standing. "We shall talk more in the morning."

He dragged the chair back down to the guard's station and headed for home — and Mrs. Field's Christmas pageant.

57

Shop of Monsieur Regnier, Grenelle, Paris, France 5:00 P.M., Wednesday, July 4, 1844.

Independence Day in a foreign country would be just another day, free of illuminations, or so Barnum thought as his carriage made its way outside the barriers of Paris to the little shop of Monsieur Regnier, an eminent mechanician who was said to sell a variety of mechanical instruments of interest to Barnum.

He was not disappointed, finding more than a few intricate locks, geared devices, and pulley systems that would serve him well when he returned to America. One invention in particular, a new kind of cuff for the hands, immediately brought back thoughts of Lily. If he ever found her, perhaps the cuffs would help.

The proprietor, M. Regnier, had greeted him politely, and upon learning that Barnum was American, quickly led him to a wall filled with various drawings, plates, and paintings, pointing out one in particular, an engraved portrait of Benjamin Franklin in a glazed frame adorned by thirteen metal stars affixed to the glass in an arc around Franklin's head.

"Your Mr. Franklin," said Regnier. "A great and excellent man. My father knew him."

"Really? How wonderful. Have you thought to add more stars? We are twenty-six states now."

Regnier shook his head. "I am certainly aware of that, but no. A promise to my father."

"It is certainly a treasure."

"Ah, yes, it is that, Mr. Barnum, but it is also much more."

"How so?"

Regnier glanced at the clock on the wall. "Mr. Barnum, if I may be so bold, you are an American far from home, and certainly far from your hotel at this hour. If you take supper with me and my family, I will show you an illumination worthy of this day, and one you will remember forever."

"Why, Monsieur Regnier, you would make a fine showman. You have me fully intrigued by your generous offer. I accept!"

Regnier led Barnum to the back of the shop and through a door that opened into the family's living quarters, neither humble nor elegant, but filled with the delightful smells of a supper Barnum would remark on for years to come, as fine and varied as any dishes he'd had at any *table d'hôte* in Paris.

Throughout the meal, as each sumptuous dish was replaced by yet another, Barnum could not help but think of Mrs. Stratton, the General's mother, and her distaste for French food.

"Everything is so Frenchified and covered in gravy," she had said. "I dare not eat it."

She had then settled upon something she could eat, and in fact relished, *saucisse de Lyons*, a sausage she so enjoyed that she had bought half a dozen pounds of it.

"Do you know what Lyons sausages are made of?" Barnum had asked her.

"No," she had replied, "but I know they are *first rate!*"

"Well," he had said, "they may be good, but they are made from donkeys!"

Mrs. Stratton had blanched, mouth agape, and soon enough had rushed to the window and thrown the lot of the sausages into the street, which were then confiscated by a large brindle dog, who made quick work of them.

At nine o'clock, the portrait of Franklin was fetched from the shop and positioned at one end of the dining table. Monsieur Regnier instructed his son to close all the curtains, completely darkening the room.

"What's this?" said Barnum, confused.

"Wait a moment," said Regnier from somewhere in the darkness.

And then the whole room was ablaze with light. Monsieur Regnier had connected the stars to a battery by means of wire, lighting them up bright as fire.

Barnum was stunned, and delighted. "What a remarkable illumination, sir, one worthy of this day and the memory of Franklin."

After some minutes, Monsieur Regnier ended the illumination. "We do this every year, Mr. Barnum. We may not be Americans, but we feel Mr. Franklin was a member of this family. We can do no less than honor him each year."

With that, bottles of champagne were brought forth, and a round of toasts were made to Washington, Franklin, and Lafayette.

By ten o'clock, after expressing his undying thanks to the Regniers, Barnum was back in his coach with the neatly wrapped mechanisms he had purchased, including the cuffs, and a bottle of champagne forced upon him by Monsieur Regnier, not that he needed more to drink.

He reflected on the day and the tour thus far. The General's performances had been well received on both sides of the channel, from the Rothschild's, to Buckingham Palace, to the theatres of London and Paris. His one regret was his flown angel. She would have made a remarkable act.

Perhaps it is not too late, he thought. He resolved to write a letter to Inspector Field that very night, urging him to continue his pursuit, and reinstating the reward. *I simply must have her.*

58

Whitehall Place, London, 9:40 A.M., Thursday, July 17, 1844.

Inspector Field sat at his desk, a letter from Mr. Barnum in his hand, one that he had read and reread half a dozen times, its message so welcome and unexpected. The search could continue, and Barnum had not just reinstated the reward, but increased it by an amount that made Field whistle through his teeth and smile with delight.

He glanced at his watch. Jeffries was now ten minutes late, unusual for him. He set down the letter and picked up another, a notice of promotion signed and sealed by none other than Colonel Charles Rowan, head of Scotland Yard.

There was a light knocking at the door.

"Enter," said Field, dropping the letter to the desk.

Jeffries opened the door and walked in, his face red from running. "Sorry, sir, a carriage plowed into a fruit cart, blocking my way. I've run the last few blocks."

Field motioned him to the seat in front of his desk. "Have a seat and catch your breath, man."

Jeffries sat down, drew a handkerchief from his pocket, and wiped his brow. "A hot one already."

Field nodded. "Yes, a bad day to be outdoors." He paused a few moments, waiting for Jeffries to finish his wiping. "But a *good* day for you, young man."

Jeffries looked up expectantly as Field lifted the promotion letter and handed it across the desk.

"Your promotion has come through, *detective* constable."

Jeffries gave a little shout, then composed himself. "Thank you, sir. You will not regret it, sir."

Field tapped his fat finger to his nose. "I am sure I will not. Now, the first order of business is to send you home, so you can get out of that uniform and select the clothes of a proper detective."

"Yes, sir," said Jeffries, beginning to stand.

Field motioned him back into his chair. "Wait, now. Be sure to pick clothes that are not too grand. You need to blend in, not stand out, so choose plain and well-worn clothing. Not too clean, not too dirty. Scuffed, not polished boots. A hat familiar with sweat and dust. Do you follow me?"

Jeffries nodded. "Yes, sir."

"Now, before I send you home, I want to tell you about two ongoing tasks. You shall have many duties, of course, and participate on many investigations and detections, but every moment of your free time shall be devoted to these tasks."

Field paused, waiting for some sign of recognition from Jeffries, who seemed distracted by news of his promotion. He seemed to be home already, trying on various disguises.

"Go on, sir," said Jeffries.

"You remember our search for the two women?"

"Yes, of course."

"Good. As you know, we released the woman known as Enku."

"Yes, sir, I remember."

"I am quite certain that the other one, the girl, will eventually return to find Enku, who has been mother to her for ten years."

"So I shadow Mr. Partly and his show."

Field smiled. Jeffries *was* a quick study. "Yes, exactly."

"And the second task, sir?"

Field knew Jeffries was not going to like the second task, so he tried to ease into it, giving the man a preamble to life as a detective. "You know, Jeffries, when I was first made a detective some years ago, I thought every day would be an adventure, rushing about London, tracking down criminals, and quickly solving cases."

Jeffries beamed. "Yes, sir."

"But it is not like that. Oh, some days are exciting, even *adventurous*, but the everyday life of a detective is like slogging through mud, searching in vain for something that never seems to appear, or appears at a snail's pace."

"Yes, sir, I realize that."

"So, the second task is just such a slogging. I want you to read as many newspapers as you can each day."

"Oh?"

"You will be looking for stories about missing and mutilated chickens or other *larger* farm animals."

Jeffries looked puzzled. "I understand about the chickens, sir. The girl, right? But why larger animals? Has she changed her preferences?"

Field shook his head. "No, we seek a third suspect, a burly man who dresses in black, also of the pale persuasion."

"What, another one?"

"Yes," said Field, twirling his finger in the air. "One who *flies*."

Jeffries gulped.

PART FIVE

I count those years with the Darwins as among the happiest of my life, although at times, as I have told you, it felt like I had traded one cage for another, from one made with bars of iron to one with bars made of manners, constraints, and the corset of expectations. Still, I had a great affection for them, and they for me. Yes, there were times when I felt like a guinea pig as Mr. Darwin prodded and poked for the meaning of my existence. But all in all, it was a happy time — with one exception.

— Lily, *Interview with the Dragon* (excerpt)

59

Four Years Later, Down House, Downe, 1:00 P.M., Monday, April 17, 1848.

Darwin slumped back in his chair and rubbed his eyes, weary now from several hours of peering into the microscope, studying his amazing barnacle, which he had named *Arthrobalanus* and Lily had amusingly embellished to *Mr. Arthrobalanus*.

Two sets of drawings lay before him on the desk, one a series of intricate drawings of *Mr. Arthrobalanus*, the other a series of equally intricate drawings showing Lily in repose and after transformation, with additional drawings showing the steps in her transformation—how her wings unfolded, how her jaw transformed into a snout, how her talons and teeth grew, and most important, how the barnacles on her forehead emerged and moved, seemingly controlling the whole process.

He popped two little blue opium pills into his mouth and waited for them to take effect. After five minutes, he popped in two more, the little pills having less and less effect on his pain and intestinal distress. Emma had urged him to seek other remedies, to "take the waters," and perhaps he would, but for now his work was too important.

He glanced at a now withered dark red balloon on the corner of his desk, and smiled. It was one of a score he had purchased in London to celebrate Annie's seventh birthday last month. Annie had been delighted, as had Willie, George, and little Bessy, just ten months old. But if they had been delighted, four-year-old Henrietta, whom he had nicknamed "Trotty" after a character in Dickens' *The Chimes*, was over the moon, racing around the grounds with a balloon until she had slumped to the ground and fallen asleep, the balloon clutched to her chest as if it were a favorite kitten. Brodie, her nurse, had eventually scooped her up and taken her off to bed.

The sound of the pianoforte in the next room, which had soothed him somewhat for the past hour, suddenly stopped. *Ah,* he thought, *the lesson has ended.*

He pushed back from the desk, steadied himself — the opium had a somewhat dizzying effect when it first took hold — and walked down the hall to the drawing room, where he found Emma, Lily, and Annie huddled around their new piano teacher, Frédéric Chopin, a Polish composer and pianist of some note, fled from Paris and the disturbing revolutions that had been underway since February.

Save for his beak-like nose, which dominated his face, Chopin was a singularly handsome man, with piercing gray-blue eyes and dark brown hair to his shoulders, which Darwin surmised had been grown to that length to provide a bit of drama to his performances, the hair whipping around and covering his face as his hands danced across the keys with amazing grace and dexterity. For all that, he was clearly a sickly man, so thin and wan that his clothes seemed to weigh him down, perhaps even outweigh him, and with a wracking cough that sometimes forced him to stop mid-chord and draw a stained handkerchief from his pocket, holding it over his mouth until the paroxysm had passed. At thirty-eight, he was just a year younger than Darwin.

Darwin smiled at him. "How are your pupils progressing, sir?"

"Comme ci, comme ça," he said, waggling a hand in the air. "Some minor problems with tempo and technique, but they improve."

"To hear Monsieur Chopin play is a revelation," said Emma, now six months pregnant with their seventh child, a boy or girl they had already decided to call Francis or Frances, depending on the outcome. "I had no idea fingers could move so expertly."

"You are too kind," said Chopin.

"No, it is true," insisted Annie, still the apple of her proud father's eye. He loved all of his children, but as he had recently confessed in a letter to his cousin William, "More than any of the other children she treats me with a spontaneous affection that touches me deeply; she likes to smooth my hair and pat my clothes into shape, and is by nature self-absorbedly neat and tidy, cutting out delicate bits of paper to put away in her workbox, threading ribbons, and sewing small things for her dolls and make-believe worlds."

Chopin gave her a curt bow. "Thank you, mademoiselle."

Darwin noticed that Lily, now fourteen and coming into her womanhood, seemed disinterested in the conversation, even distracted, looking out the window. "Lily, do you agree with Annie?"

She seemed startled, but quickly added, "Oh, yes, Monsieur Chopin is a miracle on the keyboard. I fear I shall never master it."

"*Non*," said Chopin, "the miracle is you. I cannot tell you, Monsieur Darwin, how quickly she grasps techniques. She may outdo me one day."

Darwin beamed at Lily. "What say you to that, Lily?"

"I fear I will never be so sophisticated. You play with such passion."

Chopin frowned. "The notes require little sophistication or passion, dear one. In the end, remember that *simplicity* is the final achievement. After one has played a vast quantity of notes and more notes—practice and repetition, you see—it is simplicity that emerges as the crowning reward of art."

Practice and repetition, thought Darwin, *means money and more money*. He wondered how much longer he would have to pay the man, who had demanded a guinea for an hour of instruction, a sum that Darwin had balked at, but to no avail. Emma wanted lessons from this man, and Darwin could not deny her or the girls.

"What is the name of that tune you were playing?"

"I call it opus sixty-four, number one, *Valse du petit chien*."

"Waltz of the little dog?"

"Oui, my inspiration was a little dog chasing its tail. Funny, no?"

"Yes, very amusing, and now I will forever imagine that when I hear it played."

Emma interrupted. "Monsieur, I thought it was known as the Minute Waltz."

"Yes, but it is more about petit—how you say, *miniature*."

"Oh, I had no idea," said Emma.

"Besides," said Chopin, "It takes more than a minute to play. I am not sure even *my* fingers could move that fast."

Chopin rose from the piano bench. "Now, if you will pardon me, I must to my carriage."

"Another lesson, mayhaps?"

"No, monsieur, as I have already told Madame Darwin, on my way here, I came upon a traveling show of many vans promoting various extraordinary acts, including a child who is said to play the pianoforte with his feet. I did not have time to stop, but now I shall. You and your family should come. It is only a few miles."

"Can we, can we?" squealed Annie.

Emma saw her husband's reaction and took Annie by the shoulders. "No, Annie, not today."

Darwin nodded. He had work to do with Lily, and he didn't want Emma to undergo the jostling of a carriage ride. "Mother is right, Annie, we have other plans for the day."

Annie sat down on the piano bench and crossed her arms. "We never do anything fun."

"Now, Annie," said Darwin, "mind your manners."

Annie glowered back, but Darwin ignored her, turning once more to Chopin and rolling his eyes. "Children, yes?"

Chopin smiled. "Yes, perhaps another time, Annie."

Annie said nothing, turning her back on them, causing Chopin to roll *his* eyes and whisper to Darwin, "Enfants tenaces, eh? Stubborn children."

Darwin whispered back, "Strong willed, yes, and clearly tired. Come, I will walk you to your carriage."

They walked toward the door, Darwin looking back at Lily, whose lips were trembling.

60

Three miles east of Downe, 2:15 P.M., Monday, April 17, 1848.

Chopin could not disguise his disappointment and disgust. The boy who was said to play a pianoforte with his feet was a pure sham. Two pianofortes had been employed, one that played silently without hammers, stroked without care for position or speed by the boy, and another behind a nearby curtain, obviously played by a person with some, but not much, skill.

Chopin stormed away, shouting as he went. "Faux! Imposteur! Charade!"

The proprietor of the next van beckoned him over. "Sir, I sees you is a man of some knowledge. Here, see the real thing. No tricks, I assure you."

Chopin stopped and frowned at the man. "And what could you possibly show me that is both real and extraordinaire?"

The man extended his hand. "Partly's the name, and the exotic's my game."

"Exotique?"

"Yes, I could shows you many things, a mushroom-boy, for example."

Chopin rolled his eyes. "Please, I am not stupid."

"No, sees for yourself, just over here." Partly grabbed Chopin by the elbow and directed him to a cage covered with a tarp.

"They don't like the sun, these albinos — hurts their eyes — so I covers them between shows. For their safety, you sees."

"Yes, I am certain that *safety* is your principal concern." The sarcasm seemed lost on Partly, who turned to the tarp and whipped it off, the three occupants of the cage quickly covering their eyes.

"Here, then, are my exotic prizes, sir."

Chopin stared down at them. "They do not seem that exotic."

"Oh, sir, look here," said Partly, pointing to a young boy, a dwarf perhaps, given the size of his head, with near white hair cut and trimmed all round to give the impression of a mushroom cap. "He be my mushroom-boy. Do you not see it?"

"Sir, a mushroom-boy would actually be part mushroom, would he not?"

"Well, he looks the part." Partly pointed at an even smaller child, with the same colored hair as long as her body. "Now this one, this is my unicorn child."

Chopin had to laugh. "Unicorn? What, with no horn?"

"We is between shows, sir, as I have already stated. She takes off the horn twixt shows. It itches something fierce, you sees."

Chopin shook his head in disbelief. "Why are you showing me these creatures? They are merely albinos, as anyone can clearly see."

"Well, sir, I take exception to that. As does my clientele, who are sore amazed to see them perform."

Partly pointed at the third albino, a middle-aged woman with hair teased into an explosion, naked but for a few scraps of cloth, and painted with stripes. "Now, here is the piece of the resistance, if I may say so, none other than Walla-Walla, the White Witch of Wongo-Bongo."

Chopin knelt down to take a closer look. "She is a white African, to be sure, but nothing more."

"But she be rare, sir, and from Wongo-Bongo."

Chopin stood back up and rolled his eyes. "Pathétique. There is no such place."

Partly did not know how to respond. "But, sir, they is albinos, and rare, and exotic."

Chopin frowned at him. "No, if you want to see a rare and exotic albino, I would direct you to a manor house not three miles down the road, where you will find a teenaged girl as exotic and beautiful as any albino you are likely to see, one who plays the pianoforte in the bargain."

Chopin turned and stormed away, Partly trailing behind him, holding out his hand, trying to coax some coin, with no result.

Never put the show before the coin, Enku thought, *or so Mr. Barnum used to say.*

She watched them go, her whole body shaking. *Could it be? Could she have finally found her dear Lily?*

The mushroom-boy rubbed her shoulder. "Are you all right, mum?"

"Yes," said Enku. "Get some rest now, we has another show this hour."

The boy frowned. "Mum, I am tired of being a mushroom."

The little girl chimed in. "Try being a unicorn, then. You would be a'scratchin' all day."

"Would not."

"Would, too."

Enku gave them a hard look, shushing them. "We is what we is."

61

Drawing Room, Down House, Downe, 2:30 P.M., Monday, April 17, 1848.

Emma snapped the book closed mid-sentence, startling Darwin, who was quite enjoying her reading of Dickens' latest novel, *Dombey and Son*.

"Charles, we need a governess again."

Darwin rolled his eyes. "That again? Emma, how can we afford it?"

"How can we *not*, Charles? Would you have Annie behave as she did today in front of Monsieur Chopin? It was embarrassing, and I fear she will never find a husband with so little knowledge of the social graces."

Darwin shook his head. "But I thought we agreed to grant our children some level of freedom, so they can be who they were meant to be."

"We did, Charles, but I think *old maid* is not our hope for Annie, Etty, and little Bessy."

"But the cost."

Emma sighed. "I cannot believe I am saying this, but we could save enough by discontinuing our lessons with Monsieur Chopin."

Darwin smiled. "Do you really think?"

"Yes, Charles, and I have the very candidate, a young lady of great accomplishment, Miss Catherine Thorley, who comes highly recommended. She is nineteen, is fluent in French, is no stranger to botany, and could school our little hellions *and Lily* in the arts, sciences, and social graces."

"Again, at what cost?"

"Just fifty pounds a year, Charles. Why, we are near that figure already with Monsieur Chopin."

It was true. Coin was flowing full force from the household in the specific direction of that genius of the pianoforte.

Darwin nodded. "Very well, then. Make the necessary arrangements."

Emma smiled. "Wonderful! Now, shall we get back to our book?"

Darwin stood and smoothed his waistcoat. "No, I think not. Have you seen Lily lately? I need to take more measurements."

Emma frowned. "Charles, I did not mind your measurements when she first arrived, but now, as you can clearly see, she is changing, in a womanly way."

She was indeed. "There is no need for jealousy, Emma."

"But she is so beautiful, Charles, and growing more so by the day."

Darwin relented. "Very well, today will be the last measurements I take. However, perhaps your Miss Thorley can be trained to take them in my stead, assuming she can be discreet. The science is that important."

Emma was relieved. "I think she will be happy to do so, and I will certainly make clear to her that these measurements will be part of her duties. Discretion shall be a condition of her employment."

"Good, now where is that young lady?"

"Miss Thorley?"

"No, of course not. Lily."

"I think she is in the summer house with Annie."

"Ah."

Darwin bid Emma farewell and walked the short distance from the manor to the summer house, a small structure they had built the previous year. Lily and Annie were sitting on the floor, playing pretend with Annie's dolls.

Annie saw him first. "Come, father, you can be Baby Priscilla." She held up a doll for him.

"Oh, I would love to be Baby Priscilla, but another time, Annie. Lily and I have some work to do."

"Again?" said Lily. "How many measurements do you need?"

"Many, at least until you stop growing. All part of discovering you."

Lily sighed. "I feel over-discovered."

Darwin chuckled. "Now, now, come along, my study awaits."

"Does she really have to leave, father? We were about to marry off Limping Betty."

Darwin looked down at the poor doll, whose leg had been ripped off by one of the dogs. "Well, I think we shall have to postpone the wedding, at least for an hour or so. Now, off you go to the drawing room. Mother needs you."

Annie sighed. "Very well." She put down the doll she was holding, gave Darwin a quick hug, and raced away.

Darwin turned to Lily. "Here, give me your hand."

Lily held out her hand and Darwin grasped it, pulling her to her feet. Emma was certainly right: Lily was growing fast. She was already a head taller than Emma, and near as tall as Darwin himself. She was clearly on the cusp of womanhood, her breasts and hips still mere suggestions of her future self, but alluring nonetheless. She reminded him of a partially inflated balloon, just a few puffs away from perfection, and he feared if he let go of her hand now, she would float away.

62

Whitehall, London, 3:00 P.M., Monday, April 17, 1848.

Detective Sergeant Jeffries sat at his desk, pondering the large map on the opposite wall. Over the past four years, the number of pins had grown to over two hundred, or roughly one missing or mutilated sheep a week.

The pattern of attacks remained elusive. He had used different colored pins for each day of the week, had plotted time of attack, day of attack, and distance between attacks. The only thing clear by the pattern created by the pins, which formed a ring around London, was that the attacks occurred on farms.

The latest attack had occurred at a small farm near Chartwell — one sheep missing, blood and small clumps of wool found under a nearby tree. The farmer had seen nothing, heard nothing. The sheep was simply there one minute and gone the next.

Trees, thought Jeffries. He skimmed his notebook, looking for the number of times evidence had been found under trees. The answer was sixty four, all related to daylight attacks. *He does not like the sun.* Nothing new, just confirmation that the man in black was an albino, which they had known from the start. *But if he does not like the sun, why does he attack during the day at all?*

He needed a new map, one that separated attacks by day and night. Perhaps the new map would reveal a pattern. In the meantime, "The Shepherd," as he was now known around the station, had other work to do. A new pickpocket ring had suddenly appeared near London Bridge, as usual employing young ragamuffins who had escaped from workhouses. They were clearly well-trained and highly skilled, indicating a guiding hand. The question was *who* that person was and *where* he and the boys lurked. Inspector Field had been watching his progress on the investigation, and Jeffries wanted nothing more than to please the man who had made him a detective constable just four years earlier. Jeffries had quickly proven his worth, and Fields had come through with a second promotion for him. Jeffries knew if he solved either case, he would be well on his way to full inspector.

He checked his watch. Time to check in with the detective constables he had stationed near the bridge, hoping to catch one of the pickers in the act.

As he pushed himself to his feet, Detective Constable Graves walked in and deposited a tall stack of newspapers on his desk. "Mostly news of the troubles in France, sir, but maybe some sheep as well."

"Thank you, Graves. Nasty business, that."

Graves nodded. "Too many damned revolutions, if you ask me."

"Well, at least it is not happening here."

"Yes, sir," said Graves. He looked down at the newspapers. "Would you like some help with them, sir?"

Jeffries smiled to himself. He liked Graves, a man much like himself, ambitious almost to a fault. "That would be great. Sort the clippings by sheep and chickens, and I shall take a look at them upon my return."

"Off to the bridge, then?"

"Yes, the damned bridge."

"Well, good luck, sir."

Jeffries grabbed his hat, took a few steps toward the door, then stopped. "Graves, see if you can find a new map, a fresh map."

"Yes, sir."

"And if you have time, paste it to the wall. I need to separate day attacks from night attacks."

"Would you like me to begin pinning?"

He really is ambitious, thought Jeffries. "Yes, that would be a great help. My notebook is in the top drawer. Work backwards from the most recent attacks. Perhaps we shall find the pattern that has been eluding us."

"Yes, sir, will do."

Jeffries nodded and turned for the door. Perhaps something would come to him on his walk to the bridge.

63

Down House, Downe, 3:15 P.M., Monday, April 17, 1848.

Emma was right: Lily was blossoming, her beauty distracting him as he took and recorded the measurements documenting her growth and the various steps of transformation. He would have to take them one last time, perhaps two, of course, to train the new governess. It would be critical that her measurements be taken with the same precision as his; otherwise the data would be corrupted.

Lily moved through the transformation with typical control, pausing at precisely the point where she knew Darwin would need to measure, then moving on to the next measurement. He seemed particularly interested in two things: the articulation of her jaw and the way it unfolded into a snout, and the precise time the barnacles on her head began to emerge and pulse. He was not sure yet whether the barnacles controlled the transformation or whether they were just an outcome of that transformation. He had long ago figured out how her wings emerged and unfolded from twin cavities on her back. Likewise, her tail, which uncoiled from a pocket at the base of her spine, and was extended or withdrawn using a distinct group of muscles not found on any human.

Darwin took his last measurement, snapped the journal shut, and locked it in his desk. Lily knew from long experience that the snapping of the journal was her signal to reverse the transformation, which through practice, she had learned to do in mere seconds.

Darwin watched her emerge as a beautiful young woman again, and quickly looked away from her nakedness.

"Charles, is something wrong?"

Darwin kept his back to her. "No, no. You may get dressed now, Lily."

She began tugging on the clothes she had grudgingly agreed to wear, all of which were either impractical or uncomfortable. She had been scolded more than once about throwing them off and running naked through the gardens or, a worse offense, tugging on Mr. Darwin's trousers, which were infinitely more practical and comfortable than the corsets that near took her breath away. Not even Mr. Partly had been this cruel.

"Why will you not look at me?"

"You are becoming a woman, Lily. It is not appropriate."

Lily looked puzzled. "But why? It is just my body, and you have seen it hundreds of times before."

"You are flowering, you see, and oh, perhaps we should talk with Emma. I am certain she can explain it much better than I."

Lily shrugged. "As you wish. It just seems odd."

"Yes, perhaps it is, but to the point, we have decided to hire a governess."

The word was new to her. "Governess?"

"Yes, a young woman, a Miss Thorley, who will help Emma with the raising and education of our children—and you, of course."

"I do not understand."

Darwin sighed. "It is important that you and Annie and the other girls become accomplished in French, mathematics, and the arts. And, of course, the social graces."

"Social what?"

"*Graces*, Lily. How to behave as a refined lady in this world. How to comport yourself in various social settings. To know your place, you see."

Lily looked even more puzzled. "And what will she teach the boys?"

"Why, there are social graces for boys and men as well. A man's responsibilities and duties, his place as master in the world, and how to treat women."

"Master? Like Mr. Partly and his cages?"

Darwin did not know how to respond. "Perhaps you are right. We shall have a talk with Emma, who has a much better ability than I to set things down clearly."

"Again, as you wish. You can turn around now."

Darwin turned around, pleased to see her in the flowered yellow dress Emma had had made especially for her, with secret pockets and folds that allowed her to transform without the necessity to undress, an emergency measure, Emma had called it, and a frugal measure as well. If Lily transformed in a regular dress, she would no doubt tear it to pieces, and be naked in the bargain.

"Now then," said Darwin, smiling at her. "You may return to play with Annie."

Lily didn't move. "I have a request."

"Yes?"

"Monsieur Chopin mentioned that he had seen the traveling show on his way here this morning. I am certain that she is there."

Darwin rolled his eyes. "Enku again? Lily, we have been over this time and time again. I assure you I visited that show several times over the past few years, even talked to your Mr. Partly. There was no Enku then, and there is no Enku now. She has vanished."

"No," said Lily, emphatically. "I can smell her."

"What, from three miles away?"

"Yes, she is there—*now*."

The scientist in Darwin awakened. "Really? Here, let me look in your nose."

Darwin started to touch her nose, but Lily pulled away. "No, another time. We must go there *now* and retrieve her."

"Lily, even if she is there, perhaps that is where she wants to be. If not, why in all these years has she not sought you out?"

"Perhaps she has. How would she know I was here?"

Darwin sighed. "Very well, we shall go."

"Yes!" Lily squealed.

"But not now. It is already too late to make the trip there and back before dark. We shall set out in the morning."

Lily danced up and down. "At first light?"

Darwin chuckled. "After breakfast, more like."

Lily gave him a big hug. "Thank you, Charles, thank you."

Darwin patted her gently on the back, trying not to react to the strangely exhilarating feeling of holding her in his arms. "Hold your thanks, my dear. I fear your nose is wrong."

She pulled away from him and giggled. "No, my nose knows."

Darwin wondered whether she would be right, and if right, how he would explain Enku to Emma.

64

Outside the manor house, Oxford Street, Saint Giles, London, 9:20 P.M., Monday, April 17, 1848.

Inspector Field and Charles Dickens had been walking in silence for upwards of an hour, Field struggling to keep up with the brisk strides of Dickens, who as usual was trying to walk himself into exhaustion so he could sleep, if only for a few hours.

At forty-three, Dickens was seven years younger and a head shorter than Field, but moved with greater ease, Field already burdened by the aches and strains of advancing age. Where Field was burly, he was thin, with an oblong face Field likened to a potato with a shock of long brown hair, already receded well up his forehead. His eyes were golden brown and danced when he spoke. His fame was unquestioned, so much so that Field had moved from deferential to all out obsequious where Mr. Dickens was concerned.

Field broke the silence. "There it is," he said, pointing at the manor, dark except for a faint light coming from an upstairs window.

Dickens slowed. "What?"

"That's where my Detective Sergeant Jeffries started his chase to capture that Abyssinian albino I told you about."

"Are they not called Ethiopians these days?"

Field did not like to be challenged, but he always made exceptions for Mr. Dickens. "Yes, as you say, the *Ethiopian*. He spotted her coming out of that basement window."

Dickens nodded. "I have to say, the whole story of her and the flying dragon-girl is a bit fantastical."

"For some, yes, but those of us who saw her, how she changed at the Royal Pavilion, we knows what we seen."

"I am sure you do, but I hear that this Mr. Barnum is quite the trickster, with a long history of humbugs."

Field held his fat finger next to his eyes. "I am a detective sir, and my eyes cannot be fooled."

"So you say, but to me this is more a story of interest to my American friend Edgar Poe. You are familiar with him, no doubt."

Field wasn't. "Um . . ."

"Really? You have not read *The Raven*? It is based on my own pet raven, Grip, you know, from *Barnaby Rudge*."

"Oh, how interesting. I shall try to find it at the shops."

"You should, it is quite chilling."

"I will, I will," said Field pointing down an alley. "If we go this way, we can pass through Saint Giles Cemetery and be at the station in ten minutes."

"No rush," said Dickens, turning with Field and striding down the alley. "So, any luck finding the dragon-girl or that other albino, the mysterious man in black?"

Field sighed. "Not so far, although I have a good man on the case."

"Jeffries?"

"Yes, the very one, and I feel he is close to solving the riddle of their whereabouts. Sheep continue to go missing."

"And chickens?"

"No, the missing chickens have mysteriously stopped, like she has had a change of diet, or more likely, settled comfortably in one place."

"I see," said Dickens, picking up the pace as they entered the cemetery.

They walked on in silence until they had cleared the last gravestone and rounded the corner of the church, then Field thought to change the subject. "I must say, I thoroughly enjoyed *Dombey and Son*, as did Mrs. Field. The last installment was so good we clamored for more."

"Thank you, inspector. Now, shall we go straight or walk by the *Goat and Lion?*"

"The public house, I think." He took Dickens briefly by the elbow, pointing him down the alley that led to the public house. "So, if I may ask, have you settled on a new project to delight us?"

"I have indeed."

Field waited for more, but when the silence had stretched on for several strides, he had to say, "Can you tell me more?"

"Ah, Inspector Field, you know I do not like to talk of my ongoing projects."

"Indeed, sir, but just a *taste*, perhaps, something I can share with Mrs. Field?"

Dickens relented. "Very well, I can tell you that the first installments are scheduled for next year, perhaps in May, a work to be entitled *David Copperfield.*"

"How wonderful, and I do so love your gift for naming your characters. It is a delight I share with Mrs. Field, who is avid, sir, *avid* about your books."

"Thank you, and I can tell you something else. With all this talk of albinos, I shall include one in the new book."

"I can hardly wait. Now, mind your step. They heaps garbage high around here."

Field directed him around the garbage and past the *Goat and Lion*, where a group of staggeringly drunk men were lined up against the wall of the pub, pissing in golden streams. The smell of piss and ale mixed with the smell of garbage was overwhelming, forcing Dickens and Field to cover their noses and mouths and rush on.

When they had put the pub behind them, Field continued. "And if I may ask sir, what will this albino be like? Will he be hulking, and fly?"

Dickens chuckled. "No, Inspector Field, we have worse *wingless* monsters right here on these streets and dens and dark holes to be thinking about flying beasts."

"Indeed."

"But he *will* be a villain of the first order, he will be far from hulking. More like a cadaver, thin as a new icicle with a heart to match."

"And what name will you give him?"

Dickens looked back at the *Goat and Lion*. "Well, given our most recent *experience* back there, I think the name *Uriah Heep* might serve."

It took Field a few seconds to sort it out, but then he had to stop and laugh out loud. "Oh, sir, that will serve indeed."

The bells of Saint Giles chimed half nine.

65

Whitehall, London, 10:00 P.M., Monday, April 17, 1848.

Detective Sergeant Jeffries was tired to the bone and knew he should go home, but the new map had intrigued him ever since he got back from checking in on his men at London Bridge. The pickers had marked them somehow, and there had not been a one of them to be found. With no results to show for their efforts, he had ordered his men away from the bridge, with instructions to meet the next morning here at the Yard.

The new map, showing night attacks with red pins and day attacks with yellow pins, seemed to suggest a spiral that started in Central London and then wheeled outward counterclockwise to the fields and farms around the city. Detective Constable Graves had gone a step further, highlighting the last three attacks, both in day and in night, marking the map with blue pins where he thought the next attacks might come.

Jeffries had been staring at those blue pins for hours now, with no Graves to explain the reasoning behind them, which was completely eluding Jeffries. He thought to go home, and wait for Graves to explain it to him in the morning, but then something caught his eye, a pattern within the pattern, which placed the next likely attacks far from the sites suggested by Graves.

"Of course," he shouted, startling Constable Smythe, who had been dozing at his desk. Jeffries glanced at the clock, grabbed his hat and his lamp, and raced for the door.

Constable Smythe shrugged and quickly nodded off again.

It was too late to use an official carriage, so Jeffries raced two blocks to the Royal Arms Hotel, where he knew carriages would be queued up to handle the needs of late night revelers. The only carriage in line was an old barouche-landau, not the swiftest of carriages, but the horses looked strong enough. After brief haggling about the fare—"The fare be damned, sir!"—they were racing through the streets of London, the gaslights coming quicker and quicker and then disappearing altogether as they made their way into the deep darkness of the countryside.

Jeffries knew he had broken protocol—he should have waited to discuss his findings with Inspector Field, and then set out with a troop of men to find and capture the beast, but these feedings only came once a month at best, and he was determined not to miss this chance.

The carriage suddenly slowed, the horses going from gallop to trot. "What's the matter?"

"Nothing," said the driver. "I must needs slow them in this darkness. The horses, you see."

"Of course. But as fast as you dare, sir."

"Not to worry, we is almost there. See the light in the farmhouse up ahead?"

Jeffries looked left and right, finally catching sight of the light flickering through a stand of trees to the left and perhaps no more than a hundred yards away. "Just a little closer, if you please."

"Yes, sir." The driver slowed the horses even further, finally bringing them to a halt about fifty yards from the farmhouse.

Jeffries checked his lamp, drew and cocked his pistol, and stepped from the carriage. "Wait here," he whispered to the driver, who seemed alarmed at the sight of the pistol. "Do not worry, I am a detective. Now, keep your horses as quiet as possible."

"I shall try," said the driver, "but they is jittery, a little spooked."

"Do your best." Jeffries moved away from the carriage several yards, then stopped and listened. Between the whinnying sounds of the horses he could just make out another sound coming from the left of the farmhouse, just out of the light cast by its windows.

He lit his lamp and directed its beam toward the sound. Something huge with wings and a thrashing tail was tearing into the back of a sheep, devouring it in great gulps, blood and entrails dripping from its maw. Jeffries raised his lamp to get a better look, pistol at the ready. The beast stopped and looked directly at him, sending chills up his spine.

Pain came next, followed by a light far brighter than his lamp, and then darkness.

66

Three miles east of Downe House, Downe, 10:00 A.M., Tuesday, April 18, 1848.

Darwin's manservant, Joseph Parslow, coaxed the horses on, moving them at a trot at Darwin's insistence, and not at a gallop, despite Lily's persistence that he do so. This carriage ride was Darwin's first encounter with the madness and delight of being in the company of an overexcited, squirming teenager, albeit a special one.

Emma had wanted to dress her up in a fine gown, but Lily had been obstinate, refusing to change out of her drab though flowered beige dress. She was uncomfortable as it was, and spent the entire ride adjusting crinolines and tugging at the whalebone staves along her ribs.

"Honestly, Charles," she grunted. "If I had my way, I should much prefer trousers and a waistcoat to this, this abomination." She eased herself up, twisted her dress around once more, and settled back down beside him. "Are we there yet?"

Charles chuckled. "No, my dear, but soon." He shouted up to Parslow. "Anything yet, Joseph?"

"Yes, sir, just ahead, a line of carts and vans."

"The one we want," said Lily, "has a picture on its side, Mr. Parslow."

"They alls has pictures, Miss Lily."

"A picture of a wild woman, Walla-Walla, the White Witch of Wongo-Bongo."

"Ah," said Mr. Parslow, "I sees it."

The carriage slowed and finally stopped twenty yards away from Mr. Partly's van, where a small crowd was slowly dispersing from what must have been an early morning performance.

A man on the back of the van was shouting at them. "Come back at half eleven and you shall sees further wonders to delight and amaze."

Darwin watched Lily cringe at the sound of the man's voice. He moved to get up. "Wait here, my dear."

"No," said Lily, trying to rise. "I want to see my Enku."

Darwin held an arm against her, forcing her gently back into her seat. "If what you have told me about him is true, he will most likely try to claim you as property. We do not want that, do we?"

Lily shook her head. "No, of course not, but be forceful. He is a weak man at his core, all bluster."

"Do not worry. If Enku is here, we shall leave with her."

Lily smiled. "Go."

Darwin got down from the carriage with Joseph's assistance. "Keep her here at all costs," he whispered. Joseph nodded and stood next to the carriage steps, blocking any attempted exit by Lily.

Darwin adjusted his greatcoat and began walking toward Partly's van, which in addition to a faded picture of the fearsome Walla-Walla, featured a freshly painted picture of what looked like a boy with a mushroom for a head. *Unbelievable.*

Mr. Partly caught sight of Darwin and his fine carriage almost immediately, hopping down from the van and closing the distance between them, his hand extended in greeting.

"Welcome, sir, to my amazing show."

He clearly does not remember me, thought Darwin. He reached out and reluctantly shook his hand. "Good Morning, sir."

"Our performance just ended, sir, but for the right amount, say two bob, I woulds give you and your lovely daughter a right fine private tour."

Darwin glanced over his shoulder. Lily was trying to get out of the carriage, but Joseph seemed to have her under control. When he turned back, he could see Partly squinting into the sunlight, trying to get a better look at Lily. Darwin moved in front of him, blocking his view.

"Not my daughter, and she has no interest in such a tour."

Partly tried to peer over Darwin's shoulder. "Be she an *albino*, sir?"

Darwin shook his head and forced a laugh. "*Albino*? Why, no, sir. She is my Swedish niece."

"You don't say. I hears they be like that, so pale—and lovely, sir, quite lovely."

"Yes, and let me be clear. I also have no interest in your tour."

Partly looked puzzled. "Oh, and why not? You have comes all this way for what, then?"

Darwin began his planned deception. "I have heard from others that your show features an albino, a white African."

"So?"

"I am a scientist, you see, and have a special interest in African albinos."

"Well, if you sees one, lets me know. My African albino has right fled in the night, and good riddance to the old hag."

Darwin was stunned. "Fled?"

Partly shrugged. "Gone, vanished."

"I see," said Darwin, turning to leave.

Partly grabbed him by the arm. "But I has *others*, sir. No African, mind, but albino wonders that mights delight your curiosity."

"No," said Darwin, tugging Partly's hand away. "My interest is *solely* in African albinos."

Partly seemed deflated. "I has a mushroom-boy, albino straight through, and a dwarf in the bargain."

"No, sorry."

"And a sweet young albino girl, who I has fashioned into the very image of a unicorn. Come, I shall show you."

Darwin stood his ground. "No, again."

Partly sighed and dropped his hands to his sides. "Well, then, I bid you good day, sir."

Darwin nodded and walked away, trying with each step to figure out how he would break this news to Lily.

Partly watched him go, holding a hand to his brow and squinting into the sun, trying to get a better view of the girl. "Swedish, my pink arse," he mumbled to himself.

67

Whitehall, London, 11:00 A.M., Tuesday, April 18, 1848.

Inspector Field sat in Jeffries' chair and stared at the new map on the wall, trying his best to forget what he had seen not an hour ago at a farmhouse just outside the city: poor Jeffries mauled, his head a hundred feet from his body. *The blood!*

Field sighed and looked across the desk at Constable Smythe and Detective Constable Graves, who were staring down at the floor, not wanting to make eye contact. "Tell me again, Smythe."

Smythe lifted his head, his voice quavering. "I told you, sir, I was startled awake by the sound of DS Jeffries rushing out."

"And you saw or heard nothing more? He said nothing? And you do not remember the time?"

"Yes, sir, sorry sir."

Field shook his head in disgust and pointed his inquisitive finger at Graves. "And you, sir, how can you explain the location of the *incident* when everything about your theory suggests he should have gone to a location twice as far away, in the opposite direction?" The sound of his voice rose with each word until he was shouting.

"I cannot, sir," Graves said, sheepishly. "I thought it a sound theory."

Field took a deep breath to tamp down his anger and utter frustration. Jeffries had solved the puzzle, but then had done exactly the wrong thing. "It is not your fault, either of you, I know that. Jeffries broke protocol."

Smythe and Graves nodded but remained silent, not wishing to offer any words that might further provoke their superior.

"All right, then," Field continued. "We have two tasks for this day. Firstly, you Graves, remove your *theory pins* from the map and add in the new pin, the Jeffries pin. Then I want you to stand in front of that map and give me three potential solutions to where the beast will strike next."

"Yes, sir," said Graves.

"And you, Smythe, you will come with me to inform Mrs. Jeffries of what has transpired and provide what comfort we can to her and the two little ones. It is a hard task, perhaps the hardest, but it is time you learned."

"Yes, sir," said Smythe.

"And let me be clear, Smythe. If you ever nod off on the job again, it will be *your* head."

Smythe nodded and looked away.

"All right, let us to the tasks. And Graves, see that someone transports the body to the Willis Funeral Parlor. They do fine work, though this will not be an occasion for them to display their cosmetic skills."

"Yes, sir."

Field stopped and turned at the door. "And make sure they know to send the bill to us here."

After they had gone, Graves passed the funeral instructions along to Constable Miller, and then returned to the new map, pulling off his theory pins and adding the Jeffries pin.

He pulled up a chair opposite the map and sat down. His original theory was wrong, but why? He stared at the pins, trying his best to ignore his brain's inclination to see the same pattern as before. The new pin was completely counter to his theory. What had Jeffries seen?

He slumped back in the chair, the map staring back at him, refusing to reveal its secret.

68

The road to Down House, Downe, 12:00 P.M., Tuesday, April 18, 1848.

The ride back to Down House had been a slow and somber one. Lily had been inconsolable and at times had threatened to transform and fly away to search for Enku. Darwin had managed to stop her, but only just.

"And this *perfume!*" Lily cried. "I shall never wear it again. It is all that I can smell."

Darwin put his arm around her and patted her on the shoulder. "There, there, my child, we may find your Enku yet."

"And these *clothes!* I shall never wear the like again. They are for *women*, not me. They are worse than *chains!*"

Darwin grabbed her by both shoulders. "Listen to me, Lily," he said firmly. "Crying shall not find Enku, but a plan will."

Lily pulled his hands away. "What plan? She is gone, she *hates* me, and I shall never find her — *ever.*"

She began crying again in great sobs. Darwin pulled her over, buried her head in his chest, and began stroking her hair. "Lily, Lily, my Lily."

The carriage suddenly stopped, Darwin and Lily nearly sliding off their seats.

"What is it, Joseph?"

Joseph looked back at him, his eyes wide. "Why, sir, there be a very savage in the road."

"Where?"

"Up there, sir," Joseph said, pointing down the lane to where it curved around a copse of trees, the last landmark before Down House would come into view.

Lily saw her first. "Enku!" she shouted, leaping from the carriage and racing toward a barely dressed albino woman painted with stripes, who turned at the shout and held her arms wide, shouting, "Lily!"

69

Iranistan, Fairfield, Connecticut, 1:00 P.M., Tuesday, November 14, 1848.

P. T. Barnum stood at the top of the broad flight of steps that led to the porch and interior of his newly completed home, which he had dubbed "Iranistan" to signify "Eastern County Place", or more appropriately, "Oriental Villa."

He had wanted to build such a place, his final home, he thought, after too many years on the road. He was done with tours with the General and had amassed a fortune, certainly enough for him to retire, at least somewhat. It was time to settle down, he thought, and this little seventeen-acre property had seemed a good location, remote enough from New York City but close enough to keep an eye on his American Museum.

The house he had built was unusual to say the least. He had happened upon a similar structure in 1844, the Pavilion in Brighton, England, built by George IV, and had immediately engaged a London architect to draft plans in a similar style to meet the needs of himself, his wife, and his four daughters, aged four, six, eight, and fifteen. There would be ample accommodations for all of them, as well as large dining, entertainment, and exhibition areas.

And now, after two years of construction, the work was done, and it was truly a wonder to behold, and certainly like nothing else he had seen in America, a fanciful three-story structure, a mix of Turkish, Byzantine, and Moorish architecture, with many porches and arches, the whole thing topped by multiple onion domes and spires that seemed to pierce the sky.

This little "house warming" today would be both an announcement of his retirement from touring and a proclamation that he was far from done in the show business. He had invited public officials, newspapermen, diplomats, and celebrities, even thrown open the gates to the public in the hundreds, who now scurried about the property and the mansion to view spectacle after spectacle. There was an elephant, a camel, and his latest find, which he had dubbed "The Wooly Horse," a horse whose body and limbs were covered with thick fine hair curled tightly to its skin — a true freak of nature.

For all this excitement and splendor, Barnum had one complaint: his hand was sore and tender from shaking hands with arriving dignitaries, to the point that even the gentlest touch by lady guests made him wince. After a time, he had stopped shaking hands entirely, opting to keep his hands thrust deep in his pockets, greeting guests with a smile and a slight bow instead.

The line of arriving guests had finally dwindled to two, a newspaper reporter Barnum knew well and an African diplomat dressed in his native robes.

"Welcome to Iranistan," Barnum said, giving the newspaperman a little bow.

The newspaperman smile back. "I trust you have seen my little piece on this," he said, waving his hands at the mansion.

"Oh, yes, very humorous," said Barnum. "How did it go again?"

The man was pleased to repeat it. "I syllabled it *I-ran-i-stan*, meaning of course that you *ran* before you could *stan*."

"Yes, how droll," said Barnum, motioning the man to pass by. "Enjoy your tour, and do not forget to see my Wooly Horse."

The newspaperman tipped his hat and moved toward the door to the mansion.

Only one more to greet, thought Barnum, turning to the African, who looked familiar somehow. And then it hit him.

"Why, can it be? Are you the Abyssinian, from London?"

Biniam Sahle smiled back at him. "The very one, sir, but we are called Ethiopians now, do not ask me why. It is so political."

"As I recall, you were the envoy of your emperor. What brings you here?"

"Ah, I was reassigned to the United States and had the great good fortune to be in New York City when I heard news of this event."

"You don't say?"

"Indeed, sir. I am truly pleased to be here."

Barnum wasn't sure whether to ask the next question, but he was not a man to hold back, ever. "In your time in London, did you ever hear anything more about, you know, that albino girl, the one who scared us near to death at the theatre?"

Biniam shook his head. "Unfortunately, no, although I hear the search continues by your Inspector Field."

Barnum frowned. It had been four years now, and Inspector Field had turned up nothing, despite the reward that Barnum had offered. "Yes, although his reports have come less and less frequently. I'm afraid we've lost her for good."

"Perhaps, sir."

"You seemed keen on finding her as well. Have you given up?"

"No, not at all. When I get back to Ethiopia, I plan to entreaty the emperor for another assignment to London, where I will renew my search."

Barnum beamed. "Wonderful. Come with me. I have a little drawing room where we can talk in private. Have I mentioned the reward I'm offering for the person who finds her and brings her to me?"

Biniam Sahle smiled. "Why, no, but I would like to hear more about it."

They walked quietly across the porch and into the house, Barnum happy that he had found a new hunter, Biniam Sahle happy for the chance to hunt the girl down. He would turn her over to Barnum, collect the reward, and when the time was right, chop off her head and hands as tokens of good fortune for the emperor.

It was a good day.

PART SIX

In every life, there is at least one moment when the future lies in the balance, when the choices you make mean everything. Choose one path and your life goes on with little or no change. Choose another and everything changes, as if you have walked through a curtain and find yourself on a stage, playing a role without a script, with faceless actors moving in strange ways about you, speaking in unknown languages, seeking things you cannot possibly comprehend, and yet you must play along and adapt — or die.

— Lily, *Interview with the Dragon* (excerpt)

70

Nine years later, Barnum Residence, 10 Craven Street, Charing Cross, London, 7:00 P.M., Thursday, April 2, 1857.

Life had indeed taken a turn for P. T. Barnum. One simple mistake, an ill-advised investment in a clock company, had left him near bankrupt, with no choice but to go on tour once more, in the places where he had found success ten years before, the theatres and mansions of London.

He had arrived in late December, taking up residence in a house near enough to the major theatres and close to Scotland Yard in the bargain. He had every intention of meeting up with Inspector Field and continuing their pursuit of Lily, but first he had to make some headway on restoring his fortune.

He had brought a new act along with him, a young girl, Cordelia Howard, who had achieved some fame playing "Little Eva" in *Uncle Tom's Cabin*, along with her mother, who had also achieved some small measure of fame playing "Topsy." In the new year, they were joined by General Tom Thumb, a bit plumper with age but no less talented, and together they were soon performing at the Royal Marylebon Theatre, the Strand Theatre, and Sadler's Wells, greatly restoring Barnum's fortune one performance at a time.

On rare nights off, like this evening, Barnum would entertain friends or potential business partners, who provided welcome relief from concerns of box office receipts and the health of his actors. Despite being a self-described "showman of the highest order," he was very nervous at performances, worrying endlessly that Cordelia would forget a line or trip on the stage.

So a night off and a glass of port was a godsend, particularly when he could share it with his dear friend William Makepeace Thackeray, author of *Vanity Fair* and Barnum's favorite, *The Luck of Barry Lyndon*, a man who had changed greatly in ten years. At forty-six, he was a year younger than Barnum, but the ravages of time had taken a far worse toll on him. The thin man that Barnum had met on his first European tour had grown rotund, his once taut face now a quivering show of wattles and dewlaps. His eyes, once bright, now squinted out at the world through tiny wire-frame glasses, which gave him a sour look. His movements were slow and measured now, his quick step long gone.

Barnum lifted the bottle of port. "Another glass, Will?"

Thackeray chortled. "Of course, and more of those little sandwiches, too. And do not give me that look, sir."

"Look?"

"I see you think me fat, and look at me, I can only agree with you, but I find that the less I write, the more I eat."

"Perhaps you should write more," Barnum offered, instantly regretting it. He knew he had changed as well, his hairline far back on his pate now and invaded by gray hairs.

Thackeray gave his head a little shake, his wattles and dewlaps following. "I write, I write, but I think my flower is fading. I much prefer guttling and gorging."

Barnum thought it best to change the subject. "And who are you *reading* these days? As I recall, you had a fondness for Goethe."

Thackeray stuffed a sandwich into his mouth and dispatched it with relish. "Wonderful, wonderful sandwiches. But to your question, most people expect me to answer Charles Dickens, but I find him unreadable in the extreme. He is so opposite my realistic approach to writing. Too prone to exaggerations and sentimentality. His writing just makes me cringe."

The mere mention of Dickens brought back a painful memory. "I was once quite taken with Dickens," said Barnum, "but no more."

"So you agree with me?"

"Yes and no. I find his writing first-rate, but the man himself is despicable. Have I told you what he did to me?"

Thackeray leaned forward in his chair, compressing a generous roll of fat around his waist, which threatened to pop the buttons on his frock coat. "No, but tell me."

"Ten or eleven years ago, I endeavored to purchase the Shakespeare house in Stratford-on-Avon."

"Ah," said Thackeray, "I remember the hubbub."

"Indeed, and I was stifled in my attempt by none other than Charles Dickens, who conspired with others to outbid me, not because he had a fondness for the place, but for the simple fact that he despised me."

"How unfortunate for you."

"Yes, I had a mind to move it brick by brick to New York, where I would rebuild it as a great attraction. I would have made a fortune."

Thackeray scowled at him. "Move it? Why, I have finally found something to like about Dickens. Move the bard's birthplace? Now *that* would have been despicable."

"I certainly see your point," said Barnum, pouring him more port. "As it was, I was able to divert my money to an equal prize with the purchase of Jumbo from your zoo here. Quite an attraction, and profitable."

Thackeray laughed. "I must say, you are quite single-minded in your pursuit of wealth."

"You find that amusing?"

"No, I just cannot see myself pursuing money. Now, food on the other hand . . ." He reached for yet another sandwich, at the last second deciding on two, which he stuffed into his mouth, his neck puffed up like the blowfish recently added to the American Museum, and fully worthy of exhibition in its own right. He licked his fingers and continued. "Now, as much as I would like to stay, I fear I must to my carriage."

"So soon?"

"Yes, I am afraid so. My children's former nurse, Brodie, is stopping by and is said to be bringing cakes." He waggled his eyebrows with delight. "A wonderful woman, now in the employ of a Mr. Darwin, a naturalist I am given to understand."

"A what?"

"A scientist, you know, a studier of plants and such, and in Mr. Darwin's case, a studier of *barnacles*, if you can believe it."

Barnum shook his head. "Barnacles? Why on earth would anyone spend more than a second on such nonsense?"

Thackeray nodded. "I do not know. It seems an odd way to pass one's time. Now, off I go."

Barnum walked him toward the door, Thackeray suddenly turning back, as if he had forgotten his hat, which he had not.

"Ah," he said. "I wanted to warn you. After I leave, please lock your doors. There is a team of thieves on the loose, looking for any opportunity that presents itself. Why, they quite ravished the mansion of Baroness Rothschild just a few nights ago. A great loss of jewelry and silver."

Barnum remembered the splendor of the mansion. "The baroness? How awful. I will have to pay her my respects. She was so helpful on my first tour here."

Thackeray was already halfway out the door. "Good night, sir."

"Good night," said Barnum, closing and locking the door. *Thieves? Barnacles?* He went back to his chair and poured himself the last of the port. The sandwich tray, once heaped with sandwiches, was empty save for crumbs. *Poor Will.*

71

Docks at Liverpool, England, Friday, April 3, 1857.

Biniam Sahle, son of ousted emperor Sahle Dengle, strode down the plank of HMS *Thrush* with the confidence of a man reborn. His father had been deposed two years earlier by Tewodros II, the Elect of God, but Sahle had persuaded the usurper that he could be of value at the Court of Queen Victoria.

Tewodros II had been intrigued by Sahle's strange story of the albinos Sahle had encountered on his previous stay in England thirteen years ago, and was eager for Sahle to bring back the magic imbued in their flesh and bones.

Sahle looked back at his companions, six young warriors trained with one specific goal in mind: the capture and dismemberment of a flying albino girl, now a woman if she still lived, and as many other albinos as possible. They were Sahle's *Diragī Tewagīwochi*, his "dragon warriors." Each had mastered traditional weapons—the Qolxad, a curved dagger, and the Shotel, a curved sword resembling a scythe—but were also well schooled in the use of spears and bows, their training emphasizing moving targets, particularly flying targets.

At Sahle's insistence, they had come dressed in the strange and uncomfortable clothes of Englishmen, from boots to waistcoats to top hats, every garment black save for red cravats, the favorite color of Tewodros II.

"Gehane diragonini yasadidu!" Sahle shouted. *Chase the pale dragon!*

Six warriors raised their fists to the sky and shouted out Sahle's battle cry. Seaman and wharf rats on the docks laughed or cheered, thinking the men were expressing their happiness upon arriving in England.

They were.

72

Whitehall, London, 7:00 A.M., Monday, April 6, 1857.

Detective Chief Inspector Field sat at his desk, waiting for Detective Inspector Graves to finish the paperwork that was keeping them from leaving for the Baroness Rothschild's.

Field tapped his fat finger on the desk. "Are you finished?"

Graves looked up from the paperwork. "A minute more."

Field sighed, leaned back in his chair, and stared at the yellowed map on the wall. It was known as "The Jeffries Knot" now, a puzzle no one had solved, despite the intense interest it had drawn from new recruits and any officer seeking promotion. Not a pin had been added in the past two years, which Field took to mean the beast was no more or had at least changed its diet. What was left was a crazed swirl of pins.

Graves caught him looking. "Do you think we shall ever solve it?"

Field shrugged. "It is quite the puzzle. I only wish we knew what Jeffries had seen, although not with the same result."

"Indeed."

"So, are you done?"

"Yes, sir."

"Let us go, then, before the horses die in their tracks."

They walked outside, where a two-horse phaeton awaited.

"Not the most commodious choice," said Field, "but fast."

Field climbed on, Graves following and taking the leads.

"Where is the baroness's mansion?" he said.

"She has several, but the one we want is in Buckinghamshire," said Field.

"So far?"

"Yes, well, we have an early start, do we not? We should arrive in good time."

"Yes, sir." Graves coaxed the horses onward, both men falling silent for some time, the sound of the cobbles discouraging any attempts at conversation.

When the cobbles were replaced by hard-packed dirt, Field cleared his throat and spat to the side. "Damned dust."

"Should I slow the horses?"

"No, keep up the pace."

"Yes, sir." Graves had a thought. "I say, sir, are you aware of the reports that came in over the weekend?"

DCI Field usually reviewed every weekend report upon his arrival at the Yard, but he was so wrapped up in the visit to the Rothschild's and how he would conduct the investigation, that the reports had remained unread on his desk. "No, was there something of import?"

"Of *interest* at least."

"Well, go on, what was it?"

"Albinos, sir. Four killed and dismembered, from London Bridge to East End. Two on Saturday, Two on Sunday."

Field was livid. "And no one thought to notify me!"

"Sir, the reports did not arrive from the field until early this morning. I assumed . . ."

"Never assume. *Never!*"

"Yes, sir."

Field seethed for some minutes more, his focus on the road ahead, where a tiny block on the horizon began to grow into a stately mansion. Finally, he could not resist. "Did you read the reports? Any details?"

"Yes, all were apparently killed by a group of men dressed the same, all in black. One of the reports mentions spears and oddly curved swords."

"Spears? What on earth?" Field tapped his finger aside his nose. "Were they large men, like the one we have been seeking all these years?"

"We are not sure, sir. They were only described as tall. Oh, and copper skinned."

"Africans? Well, I guess that makes some sense. You know, the spears."

"Certainly strange business."

"Indeed." Field pointed down the road. "There, on the left, the Rothschild's."

Graves slowed the horses as they entered the gate, a man in full livery pointing the way to the front portico.

"Now," said Field. "Let me do the talking here. Your job is to observe, and learn."

"Very good, sir."

"And we shall discuss the murders further on our ride back to the Yard."

Graves nodded and dropped the reins as several footmen, all dressed in gaudily embroidered gold pantaloons and long coats, surrounded the carriage and took hold of the horses.

One of the men, clearly a servant of some rank, escorted them quietly up the steps and into the mansion, where Field had to stop a moment to catch his breath. He had never seen so much gold and silver on display. Everywhere he looked, there was something new and extraordinary to take in. He tried to remember it all, knowing that Mrs. Field would want a full accounting.

"This way, gentlemen," said the man, ushering them into a drawing room, a room of equal splendor, with ceilings so high they could accommodate a full-grown tree.

The man left, leaving Field and Graves to quietly consider the room, each spinning in place, looking high and low, mouths agape. They were so transfixed, they were not aware of the Baroness Rothschild's presence until she spoke.

"Gentlemen," she said. Her voice was high and lilting.

They broke from their reverie to take her in. If anything, she was more splendid than the room itself. She was not young by any means, but neither had she reached the point where people would describe her as handsome and not beautiful. Small wrinkles appeared at the corners of her pale blue eyes when she smiled, but no other wrinkles were evident. Her nose was narrow with a slight bob at the end, which seemed to bounce when she spoke. Her lips were painted red, and a lampblack mole had been positioned just above them on her left cheek. Brown curls done up in gold ribbons fell from both sides of her head, which was topped with a jeweled tiara.

She seemed to be dressed for a ball, not a meeting with the constabulary. Her gown was white satin, with vertical threads of silver and gold running through it as accents to green vines and roses embroidered into the dress with great care. The overall impression was of a woman emerging from a garden.

Field gulped and gave a quick bow. "Baroness Rothschild."

She nodded, seemingly amused by the man standing before her, but stifling the laugh that struggled to escape from within.

Graves bowed deeply, the baroness nodding back.

"No need to be so formal. *Baroness* will suffice."

"Yes, *baroness*. As you may recall, I am Detective Chief Inspector Field, and this is my colleague, Detective Inspector Graves. At your service." He gave another little bow.

"Yes, I remember you," she said "from that Royal Pavilion *event*. Thank you for your promptness. Now, please have a seat."

She directed them to chairs in full gilt and clearly French, chairs so beautiful Field was reluctant to sit.

From the look she gave Field, such hesitation had happened before. "Sit," said the baroness, her tone insistent, though not grating.

They sat down, the baroness taking a chair opposite them. "Will you take tea?"

Field shook his head and raised his fat, inquisitive finger into the air. "No, baroness. We would not take up so much of your time. We are here only and precisely to gather facts about your losses, so as to find the villains who have trespassed here and made off with your property."

"Nonsense," said the baroness, raising a hand and glancing back over her shoulder, signaling a man who seemed to separate himself from a wall as finely dressed as he was, and walk quickly from the room.

"You are too kind, baroness."

She smiled back at him. "Now, to the *theft.*"

Field eased back in his chair and listened as the baroness described the timing, manner of entry, and results of the crime, cataloging each and every item that had been taken and from which rooms.

By the time she had finished, a silver tray sat before them, filled with gilt-rimmed china cups of freshly poured tea and little cakes topped with pink icing and cherries.

"Now," said the baroness. "Have a cup of tea while you consider what has transpired here. I shall return in a moment."

She stood and floated from the room, a servant closing the door behind her.

Graves grabbed a cake and stuffed it into his mouth as soon as she had gone. "Oh, my, this is wonderful. You should try one, sir."

"No, thank you, but perhaps one for Mrs. Field." He pulled a handkerchief from his coat, gently wrapped it around a cake, and returned it to his pocket. "She will be quite delighted."

He turned back to Graves. "Now, what do you make of her?"

"She is quite beautiful."

"Well, of course she is. No, I meant her story?"

"Oh, I only wonder how she could possibly know what was taken. There is so much to take."

"I agree with you, but on the other hand, her servants are more likely the ones who know. After you dust something long enough, its absence is no doubt quite startling."

"Excellent point, sir. I do wonder about the scope of the theft. Items are missing from so many rooms."

"Yes, and that would take a great deal of time, in a house swarming with servants."

"Do you think it may have been a servant, then, or servants?"

Field tapped his finger to his nose. "I am thinking precisely that, and I am pleased that you have reached the same suspicion."

"We shall need to talk to each of them."

"Yes, but we will have to be circumspect. She may take offense at our suspicions."

The door swung open and the baroness floated back toward them.

"Let me do the talking," Field whispered.

The baroness sat down and smoothed the folds in her gown, finally clearing her throat and leveling her gaze on them. "So, have you considered all I have said?"

"We have indeed, baroness," said Field, "and we would learn more."

"More? I have told you all I know."

"Yes, of course, but it would be helpful to know who exactly noticed each piece that is missing."

The baroness frowned, clearly displeased. "You want to talk to my servants, is that it?"

"Yes, baroness, that would be most helpful."

She shook her head, annoyed. "But that will take time, and as you well know, time is a thief's best friend."

Field thought to remember that, for some future soliloquy aimed at his team. "I assure you, the thieves will not escape our meticulous and headlong pursuit."

The baroness was about to reply, but at that moment, Graves thought to cross his legs, his boot catching the edge of the tray, sending it and its contents into the air with a crash.

The baroness threw up her arms and gave a little shout, her expression locking a memory into place for Field. She had reacted in just the same way at the Royal Pavilion. It all came back to him. The beast flying about. People in headlong panic. The man in black. The Abyssinian with the curved sword. *Curved sword? Was he somehow involved in this new business, these murders?* And then there was the curious way the beast had sniffed at a couple in the box just below the box of the baroness. *It acted strangely, as if it knew them. Who are they?*

Graves was beside himself and in full-throated apology, not knowing whether to bow or curtsy or try to scoop up the shattered cakes. "Oh my, oh my."

The baroness quickly composed herself and rose from her chair, signaling her man for assistance, which arrived in the form of a maid, who quickly began to clean up the mess.

"I believe we are done here," she said. "I shall make the servants available to you, and provide a room for your discussions, which I hope can be carried out with some care to time."

Field bowed. "Thank you, baroness."

She turned to leave. "Good day, gentlemen."

"Baroness, if I may, a word more, on another matter."

She turned back. "Yes?"

"The Royal Pavilion."

She looked puzzled. "That *business*. We discussed that some years ago."

"Yes, but I have had another thought. A question has come to mind, you see, about the beast."

The baroness grew pale, her lips trembling, her voice a whisper. "The beast?"

He let her gather herself, and then continued. "The beast, yes. Do you recall how it landed in the box just below you?"

"Yes, it was terrifying. I so worried for the safety of Mr. and Mrs. Darwin."

Field's eyes grew wide. "Mr. and Mrs. Darwin? You did not mention them by name when last we spoke of this."

"I thought it of no consequence. It would have been unseemly for me to mention them by name."

Field turned and gave Graves a rolled-eyes look, before turning back to the baroness. "Perchance do you know where they reside?"

She shook her head. "Not really. In the countryside, I believe. Now, is there anything else?"

So, so much, he thought. "No, baroness, and thank you for your hospitality and understanding. We shall be quick about our work."

The rose garden that was the baroness turned and glided from the room.

73

Down House, Downe, 10:00 A.M., Monday, April 6, 1857.

Darwin dropped his pen on the desk and slumped back in his chair, rubbing at his eyes. Work on *The Origin of Species by Natural Selection* was proceeding apace, but it was at times like these, when he let his guard down, that memories of Annie, his joyous child, would come to him. Although she had been dead for six years, he still expected her to burst into the study and rush onto his lap.

Work had helped ease the pain. He had published four monographs on barnacles and his continuing studies on Lily had accounted for three more, although they lay locked in the desk drawer. He could not possibly publish them, at least not yet. The published monographs had gained him respect and no small measure of praise in the scientific community, which would be critical to the acceptance of this new work.

The family had also grown. Eight children, his "treasures," now roamed and wrestled in the halls and rooms of Down House: Willy, age 17; Etty, age 14; George, age 12; Bessy, age 10; Francis, age 9; Leonard, age 7; Horace, age 6; and Charles, age 1.

And then there was his darling Lily, now age 23 and fully formed. She was an inch or two above six feet tall now, and more beautiful than ever. After many years of struggling, she had finally accepted the social graces and her role as a woman in a man's world. She was accomplished in French, needlepoint, and sewing, and could hold her own in rational debate on poetry and prose. Not that this new transformation had met with universal approval. Enku, who was a mother to her, had kept pressing her to become her "true self."

What that true self was had kept Darwin up many a night as he tried to figure out how she might fit into his developing theory. Was she a new species, a freak, or something entirely new: three species occupying the same biological mass, a symbiotic colony, if you will? His eight years of work on barnacles had vaulted him to a plateau of respectability, if not the heights, in the scientific world, but had done nothing to solve the problem of Lily.

He ran a hand across his head, which was now bald save for a thatch of brown hair on each side joined at the cheeks by a graying thicket of sideburns that reached to his collar. His eyebrows, what Annie had called his fuzzy caterpillars, had grown even bushier and now were laced with gray as well. He was forty-eight years old, but felt and looked much older.

A sound behind him caught his attention. It was Emma, come to coax him for a walk along the sand path, no doubt. The years had been hard on her, too. Ten pregnancies had taken their toll, the last just a year ago, a difficult pregnancy that had produced Charles Waring Darwin, a child of strange aspect who was struggling to thrive.

"Charles," she said. "May I have a word?"

Charles knew that "a word" to Emma was often much more than a paragraph and more even than an exhaustive treatise on any given topic. He motioned her into the chair beside the desk. "Yes, of course. Is it about Charles?"

Emma frowned. "No, though we do have to talk about him as well, and soon. Something is fearfully wrong with him."

"Agreed. Now, what is causing that frown?"

Emma took a deep breath. "It is Lily, of course."

"Why Lily?"

"Oh, Charles, you know as well as I do. She is full grown, and more to the point, I see no signs of further aging, just as your Chinaman predicted."

"Emma," Charles said, shaking his head, "she is but twenty-three, in that pleasant zone where beauty thrives. It is too soon to tell whether the Chinaman was right."

Emma persisted. "But she cannot stay here much longer. Soon our own children may grow older than she. It will be noticed."

Charles sighed. "What would you have me do, turn her out onto the highways?"

Emma bristled. "Charles, you *always* go to the extreme. Now stop it, please. No, what I have in mind is a plan, a plan to marry her off."

The words stunned him. "Marry her off?"

"Yes, now please stop shaking your head and hear me out."

"Very well," he said. If there were anything more complicated than "a word," it was "a plan."

"Good, now let us assume that Lily will not age a single day more."

Charles nodded.

"That, of course, presents problems, people aging around her and so forth."

"Yes?"

"What she needs is the ability to age alone."

"What?"

"Quiet, now hear me out. If a woman wants to live alone in this world, what is the one thing she needs more than anything else?"

"An island?"

"Charles, stop it! No, she needs money, and a lot of it."

"Well, we do not have that."

Emma was growing exasperated with him. "Of course we do not. And that is my point. The only way she can get money is through marriage."

Charles was skeptical. "But how would that solve her not aging?"

Emma brightened. "That is the beauty of my plan, Charles. We will marry her off to a wealthy gentleman, someone old and without relatives. She will inherit a fortune, enough to maintain her privacy for all eternity if necessary."

Charles scratched at his sideburns. "Hmm, I can see how that might afford her *some* privacy, but wealth means a manor, and a manor means servants. How will she hide her non-aging from them?"

"Oh, Charles, do not be so dense. She keeps the servants for a time, a few years at most, and then switches them out."

Charles shook his head. "That will work for a few turns, but eventually people in the village will compare notes, will they not?"

"I have thought of that contingency as well, Charles. She simply sells the manor and moves to a new city or country, and starts over. It is a perfect plan."

Charles had to admit the plan might work. "It could work, yes, but I see no need to rush into this. Perhaps in a few years."

"No, Charles, in a few years her aging problem will be fully evident, and we would be hard pressed to initiate this plan with any success."

Charles crossed his arms and leaned toward her. "Wait, are you saying that your plan is already in motion?"

Emma cocked her head to one side and gave him a little smile. "Yes, of course it is in motion, which is why we need to talk about tonight's dinner."

"Dinner?"

"Yes, we have a special guest, none other than Sir Arthur Bambridge, baronet."

Darwin's eyes widened. "*The* Charles Bambridge?"

"The very one. Wealthy. Ninety years old. Fading. No relatives."

"And he is aware of your plan."

Emma laughed. "Of course not, but once he sees Lily, I am sure I can persuade him of its benefits."

"I am not so sure."

"Oh, you just wait, and do not tell me that if you were in the baronet's place you would not want the attention of a beautiful woman during your final days."

Darwin smiled back at her. "Point taken, but I already have such a woman."

Emma stood and punched him playfully on the arm. "Come on, you rascal, it is time for a walk in the garden. We must discuss how to make Lily aware of the plan."

And that, thought Darwin, *was exactly where the plan would most certainly go wrong.*

74

Whitehall, London, 1:00 P.M., Monday, April 6, 1857.

The trip back from the Rothschild's had been pleasant enough, except for a brief, unexpected downpour that had left the two of them soaked to the skin. Field had sent Graves home to change and had sent a boy to fetch a change of clothes from Mrs. Field. Meanwhile, he had gathered everyone for an all-hands meeting to discuss the robbery — a clear case of snatching by servants — and the new clue about the years-old Royal Pavilion case, the names of the couple in the box directly below the Rothschild's.

Information came immediately, in the form of one Detective Constable Williams.

"Sir, I know of them," he said. "My girl, Bessy, she does some cleaning for them from time to time. Messy children, you see."

"Wonderful," said Field. "Where might we find them?"

"Downe, sir. A little ways outside Downe."

Field rushed to the map, waving his finger over it until he had found Downe, a small parish in Kent, not fifteen miles to the southeast. "There!"

"We could be there quick enough," said Williams, "Swing by and pick up my girl, who will show us the way."

"When my clothes arrive, yes," said Field. "Now, where do we stand on the weekend murders of the albinos?"

Detective Sergeant McKnight called out from the back of the room and made his way through the other officers. "The murderers are still at large, but given their unique dress and appearance, we hope to have them this day."

"Who is working the case?" said Field.

"Myself, two detectives, and seven uniformed constables. They are in the field as we speak, at each of the sights, and canvassing the areas."

"Good," said Field, tapping his finger against his nose, a clear sign to the men that he had something more to offer. "Well, then, let us also send word to each station to alert them to the physical description of these men."

"Yes, sir."

"Oh, and a question. Do all the murders involve albinos?"

"Well, yes. I mean there were six other murders over the weekend, but none that seem to fit the details of the albino killings."

"All right, then," said Field, but just as quickly stopped, his finger waggling in the air silently. "Wait now, do we have a description of the weapons these men used?"

"Yes, sir, we have a few drawings gleaned from witnesses. Let me just fetch them from my desk."

Williams moved quickly to the back of the room, scooped up a sheaf of papers from his desk, and brought them forward, spreading them out on Field's desk, all the men gathering round for a look-see.

Field was already connecting the dots, the hair on the back of his neck at full attention as he took in the drawings, which showed a spear, a dagger, and most chilling, a uniquely curved sword, one Field had seen years before at the Royal Pavilion Theatre. *Could it be the same man?*

After a few taps of his finger upon his nose, Field was ready to issue orders. He scanned the room. "Where's Beakins?"

"Here, sir," said Beakins, elbowing his way forward.

"As I recall, you pride yourself on your running."

"Yes, sir, I do," he beamed. "No one can match me."

"Good. I want you to run over to the Ministry. See if they have any information about the arrival of envoys from Ethiopia."

"Yes, sir, I am on it." He grabbed his hat, making ready to leave.

"Wait," said Field. "Also the names and locations of everyone at the Ethiopian consulate."

"Yes, sir, is that all, sir?"

"Yes, now show me your speed."

Beakins pushed through the men and was gone. Field turned to the others. "Now, then, with any luck, Beakins will be back soon, and then I shall have further orders for you. Be ready to leave on a moment's notice."

The men dispersed, some with a quick nod, some with a shrug, and some in shared, whispered grumbles.

Field sat back down at his desk, wondering what was taking the boy so long. No doubt, Mrs. Field was being particular about which trousers and which waistcoat to send, and would deliver upon the boy just the right clothes for a detective chief inspector on a fine April afternoon.

The pinned map caught his attention: The Jeffries Knot. Was it possible that *everything* was connected: the flying girl, the man in black, the Ethiopians, and the Darwins? And now it was all coming together, all these years later, with the suddenness of a cymbal crash? He thought so, which made him even more impatient for the arrival of his clothes.

A voice behind him startled him. "Good morrow, Inspector Field."

Field turned and offered a broad grin. "Why, Mr. Barnum, sir, it is a pleasure. Please, have a seat." Field motioned him to a chair opposite his desk.

Barnum sat down. "Here, what's this?" he said, looking down at the drawings. "Swords and daggers?"

Field scooped them up and turned them face down on the desk. "A case."

He gave Barnum the onceover. The man had not changed all that much since he had last seen him. A bit heavier, a bit balder, but his eyes still twinkled with that same energy. "May I assume you would like to have an update on our search for the two albinos?"

"Indeed, I would."

"Your timing is impeccable, Mr. Barnum. I think we may have some new clues, some new angles, if you will, that will serve us well in the discovery and capture of said albinos, perhaps even today."

Barnum's eyes grew wide. "Tell me more," he said, leaning across the desk.

Field's finger raised itself up, leading the way.

75

Down House, Downe, 1:30 P.M., Monday, April 6, 1857.

Lily and Enku sat on Lily's bed, passing the glass-plate photograph of themselves back and forth. Willy Darwin had taken it earlier in the day, using the new equipment his father had bought for him.

He had posed them standing together in Darwin's study, microscopes and specimens on the desk behind them, and behind that, Darwin's wall of books. The sun was coming in at an angle, putting one side of their faces in shadow.

Enku looked pensive and a little blurry, having ignored Willy's admonition to remain still for the length of the photograph, her hand clearly in motion, headed for a nose that needed a scratch. She was old now and hunched, and more than a foot shorter than Lily. Her gingham dress and lace bonnet served notice that Walla-Walla, the White Witch of Wongo-Bongo, was no more.

Lily by comparison looked composed and radiant, looking out on the world with pale eyes that seemed to master all they saw. She had grown into a beautiful, statuesque woman, with a figure that couldn't be hidden behind the plain gingham dress she wore. Had Willy thought to title the photograph, "Goddess and Crone" would have been apt.

"I do not like this," said Enku, her face screwed up into a frown of distaste.

"You look fine," said Lily. "Look how your eyes catch the light."

Enku shook her head. "No, it is bad magic. I am now in two places at once. Part of me has been stolen. Do you not feel that?"

Lily laughed. "No, of course not. It is just the work of light and chemicals, and wondrous, I think."

"Magic," said Enku, crossing her arms. "We should smash it."

Lily, alarmed, took the photograph from her. "No, we must keep it safe. Just imagine, people hundreds of years in the future will know we were here, and what we looked like. It is a treasure."

"A curse more like."

Lily sat the photograph aside, placing it carefully on her nightstand. "Now, to this evening."

Enku got up from the bed and began pacing. "Do you *have* to do this? I do not like Miss Emma's plan. No, not at all."

"Nor I, but there is a logic to it, if you believe what I have been telling you."

"That you will live forever."

"No, that it is *possible* that I might live forever."

"You are right, I do not believe it. They are playing a trick on you, trying to get rid of you."

"No, Enku, they are thinking of my future, and *yours*."

"Mine?"

"Yes, you would come with me, would you not?"

Enku offered a brief smile. "Yes, I would hope to do that, to protect you from this man they have arranged." She stopped pacing and frowned down at her. "But it would be *wrong* to do this."

Lily knew where she was headed. "My *true self*, again?"

Enku sat down beside her and took her hand. "Lily, you do not remember what you were when I first saw you."

"A little beast, a terror, you said."

"But more, Lily. And hiding in fancy clothes and manners will not change that. Why, Mr. Darwin himself has told you of what is to come. And you must prepare for it. If not, I fear you shall not be ready, that that brother of yours will win out."

Lily puffed out a deep sigh. "Enku, Mr. Darwin himself does not believe all that my father told him. It is so fanciful."

"Fanciful, *fanciful?* Do you not remember the Royal Pavilion—the rage, the power? You were *magnificent!*"

"Yes, but—"

"And that was when you were *ten.* Look at you now. Taller. Stronger. Imagine what is possible, Lily."

"You are right. I was a child in a blind rage and unable to control my transformation. Now I can, and now I *only* transform in the interest of science, so that Mr. Darwin can complete his research."

Enku was enraged. "Research? You are nothing more than a guinea pig in a fancy dress of a cage. Wake up, Lily!"

Lily tried to mollify her. The argument was so tiresome. "Enough, Enku, *enough,*" she said as calmly as possible. "Now, we have but a few hours to prepare for dinner—and the baronet. Which dress shall I wear?"

"None," Enku snapped. "Go as your true self, and let him see what he has bargained for." She stormed from the room, crying.

Lily sat there for some moments in silence, then picked up the photograph—a moment in time. *What* does *the future hold?* she thought, then whispered to herself, "The flowered yellow dress, I think."

76

A field in Lewes Green, England, 2:30 P.M., Monday, April 6, 1857.

Partly was completely distracted by the freshly painted sign on his van:

Dr. Partly's Poshuns, Loshuns, and Noshuns. Fevers and agues be gone! Aches and pains be tossed! Cures for every ill! Knives also sharpened.

He was so distracted he didn't see the man in black who had come up behind him. The voice startled him.

"You are Mr. Partly, are you not?"

Partly spun around to see the face of an African staring back at him. He was dressed like a gentleman, in fine clothes, black from boot to top hat. A large group of similarly dressed men sat in a large carriage a few yards off, not a single smile among them.

"Yes, well no, I be *Doctor* Partly now." He waved at the new sign, which the African ignored.

Biniam Sahle squinted at him. "You do not remember me?"

Partly looked him up and down, then took a quick step back. "You be the Abyssinian at the Royal Pavilion."

"*Ethiopian,* yes."

"Here now, that business has been dead, what, thirteen years if it were a day."

"For you, perhaps." Biniam glanced around. There was no sign of anyone other than Mr. Partly. "So, I take it that you have not seen the flying albino, the dragon-girl?"

Partly shook his head. "Gone, vanished."

"And the older one, your white witch?"

"She came back for a while, but up and fled near nine years ago."

"So you have no albinos at all?"

"No, not a one. Well, I used to, a boy and a girl, but they has gone and fled as well, not a month ago, leaving me to seek other gainful employment in the growing field of poultices and plasters."

Biniam scanned the other vans lined along the road. "And the other penny shows. Any albinos?"

Partly scratched his cheek, thinking. "Well, now, let me see." He looked down the line of vans. "Ah, yes, Cooper's Creepies has one. No, wait, Cooper done left three days ago."

"Do you know which way he went?"

Partly scratched his head. "No, but the road only leads one way or the other."

Biniam frowned. "And you have not heard a word from the flying one?"

"No, if I had, I would be a wealthy man. Barnum's reward still stands."

Biniam's eyes widened. "You mean that Inspector Field is still searching for her?"

"Oh, yes, he is a right bulldog that man. Was here not long back, inquiring and such."

Biniam glanced back at his carriage. He could tell they were eager to attack, if only Biniam would give them the signal. He turned back to Partly and gave a little bow. "I thank you for the information and wish you the best with your new, um, *endeavor*."

"My what?"

"Your endeavor." Biniam could see that Partly was not familiar with the word. "Your *business*."

"Oh, yes, quite."

Biniam turned and headed for the carriage.

"Wait," said Partly. "I have a question."

Biniam stopped and turned back. "Yes?"

"I cans understand why you would be looking for the girl, for Lily, but why are you searching for just any albinos?"

"Ah, a fair question, Mr. Partly. Firstly, with the hope that one may know your Lily and thereby lead us to her."

"I see, and it is Dr. Partly now, by the by."

Biniam nodded and continued. "And secondly, I and my men there in the carriage are on a mission."

"What, like a religious mission?"

Biniam smiled. "You may say that. We are trying to create a new community, a town if you will, where albino men, women, and children can live free and not be subjected to ridicule or grief of any kind, most particularly as freaks at penny shows."

"I sees, I sees. A noble cause that."

"Indeed. Now, I shall bid you good day."

"Hold up a minute. I do knows of one."

"Really? Who? Where?"

Partly gave his cheek a good scratch. "This was years ago, so if she has moved on, do not blame me."

"No, of course not. A *she*, you say?"

"Yes, a man stopped at my show, and he had an albino girl, maybe thirteen or fourteen years old, with him. Said she was Swedish, but I knows better."

"And do you know this man or where he lives?"

Partly scratched again. "Yes, and no. We was outside Downe, maybe a few miles, so I assume he came from there, but where he lives exactly, I do not know. On the other hand, he was a right gentleman, so I would look, if I was looking, for a grand manor or large farmhouse."

"Thank you, Mister—um *Doctor*—Partly, and which direction is Downe?"

Partly pointed down the road. "Just head north, you cannot miss it. Maybe twelve miles, I think. Oh, but do not be surprised if the young lady does not wish your generous offer of help."

"Oh, and why is that?"

"She was a right fine young lady, dressed in a frock with frills of the latest styles. Rich, you see."

"Ah, I see. Well, thank you again." Biniam bowed and tipped his hat, a mistake that became quite evident when six arrows suddenly blossomed in Partly's chest.

Biniam raced for the carriage.

Partly fell on his back, his last breath knocked out of him, his eyes fixed on the sky. A cloud floated by that he thought looked just like his mum, except for the nose, and then the world grew dim.

77

Down House, Downe, 4:00 P.M., Monday, April 6, 1848.

Out of deference for Sir Arthur Bambridge, baronet, who usually supped at this hour so that he might doze off before sunset, the meal had been moved to several hours earlier in the day, which had been a great disruption to the Darwin household. Maids had scurried about, fetching bath-can after bath-can of water for rushed bathing. Mrs. Davies, the cook, known as "Daydy" by the children, had given up her afternoon game of whist to near melt above the stove as she prepared roasted chicken, carrots, and mash while keeping a close eye on her signature gingerbread, which she would top at the last minute with a sauce of her own making.

But finally, just a few minutes before the knock at the door, everything had come together. The children had been fed and taken off to Darwin's study for "games" with their governess, Miss Thorley, and a reluctant Nurse Brodie, leaving Charles and Emma to greet the baronet in the drawing room. Lily, of course, would be presented to the baronet in the usual display of dignified, mannerly tardiness.

Darwin, who gave the whole affair little import, had refused to bathe or even change clothes. He still wore the wrinkled brown trousers, waistcoat, and frock coat he had worn all day.

Emma had persuaded him to change out his cravat, from matching brown to what she considered a "striking" royal blue.

Emma had dressed as if for a coronation, opting for a scoop-necked emerald green gown held tight at the waist by hidden whalebone supports that created a fan effect at the bodice. White bows made of silk chiné ribbon adorned each shoulder, which had the effect of drawing the viewer's attention to her face, which still retained much of its beauty.

Darwin had opened the windows to allow a spring breeze in the drawing room, and then they had sat in silence for some minutes, waiting. Finally, there was the knock and the unmistakable approach of the baronet, his cane tapping hard on the floor as he made his way slowly down the hall, Mr. Parslow leading the way. And then they appeared.

"May I present Sir Arthur Bambridge, baronet," said Parslow with a quick bow.

Darwin rose from his chair, closed the distance, and shook the baronet's hand. "Thank you for coming." He turned to Parslow and whispered, "That will be all." Parslow nodded and left the room.

"My pleasure, I am sure," said the baronet with a nod. His voice was soft and gravely.

Darwin wondered how this "plan" was ever going to work. The man was not just old, but clearly at death's door. It was evident from his long out of style clothing — *no one wears double-breasted frock coats anymore, and certainly not in this goldish brown* — that time had shrunk a formerly robust man. The clothes seemed to overwhelm him. All in all, he was a rather plain man, neither handsome nor ugly. Bald except for a wisp of gray hair atop his head, he looked like a pale melon, his skin the color of aged parchment, with blue veins showing through like rivers on a dusty plain.

"Please have a seat, sir, and say hello to my wife, Emma, who has orchestrated this meeting."

"Ah, yes," said the baronet, raising a tightly clenched handkerchief to dab at his rheumy eyes. "I found your letter of invitation quite charming, and I see now I am met by a lady who exceeds that charm."

Emma smiled and offered her hand, which the baronet grasped softly and briefly. "You are too kind, sir. A woman my age."

The baronet would have none of it. "If you want age, my dear, look at me if you dare. I am more bones than man."

"Not at all, sir," said Emma. "Please have a seat."

The baronet looked around. "Are we only three?"

"No," said Darwin, "there is another, our ward Lily, who shall be here presently.

"A ward, you say?"

"Yes, we took her on some years ago. She was alone in the world, you see."

"How sad," said the baronet, dabbing the drool at the corner of his mouth, which ebbed and flowed as he spoke, as if some internal pump was wasting him away a drop at a time.

"Yes," interjected Emma, "but we are happy to have her, and she is quite the beauty, as you shall soon see."

The baronet eased himself into a chair and dropped back with a painful grimace. "A beauty, you say. Well, it seems that I will be doubly blessed this day. I surely hope my heart can withstand it."

As if on command, Lily appeared at the door, which caused Emma to gasp. She had never seen Lily quite this lovely. She wore a gown made of diaphanous pale yellow wool gauze imprinted with tiny red flowers and pale green leaves and woven with matching red silk stripes along the fanned bodice, which made it shimmer in the light. The dress was tight at the waist, which Emma knew had been corseted tight by Enku, and bulged outward from her hips, growing even wider as the dress fell to the floor, the work of several crinolines underneath. The dress was sectioned in flounces, which gave the effect of waves lapping on a beach or the cascade of a waterfall.

The baronet, mouth agape from the vision before him, attempted to stand, but Lily was quickly in front of him, taking his hand and urging him back into the chair. "Sir, there is no need to stand. It is I who am honored."

As the baronet squeezed her hand gently, Lily glanced out the window. Enku was in the garden, along the sand path, pacing back and forth, and looking furtively at the house. She had not liked the plan at all, and certainly not the dress, which she had likened to a disguise. Lily would have to have another talk with her; that was clear. The Darwins had been extremely kind to her, and she wanted to pay them back, even if it meant moving away, to care for the skeleton of a man before her.

"Well," said the baronet, "I am sure that is for the best, for you have quite taken my breath away." He dabbed at his mouth, which seemed to have greatly increased its flow.

Lily curtsied and moved silently to a chair opposite him, settling herself into it with practiced ease, her hands keeping the crinolines under control as she gathered them around her. She glanced out the window again. Enku was still pacing.

"Well, then," said Darwin, thinking to provide a list of Lily's accomplishments and charms.

But the scream from the garden intervened.

78

Approaching Down House, Downe, 4:00 P.M., Monday, April 6, 1857.

Detective Chief Inspector Field, Mr. Barnum, Detective Constable Williams, and his girlfriend, Bessy, had talked themselves into silence as they covered the fifteen miles between Whitehall and Downe. Bessy had offered up descriptions of two albinos living at Down House, one a young lady and the other elderly, both fitting the descriptions of Lily and Enku, although Bessy did not know their names.

The descriptions had launched Field and Barnum into a long, animated conversation about Lily, and most particularly for Field, the reward, which he sought to increase further by intriguing Barnum enough that he would offer a like reward for the man in black, should he ever be apprehended. Barnum was unsure, but was willing to discuss it further should the man actually be found and be of interest as a subject of future exhibition.

Field described their current pursuit of the man, and tried his best to explain The Jeffries Knot, but Barnum waved him off, unable to grasp the map without actually seeing it. Conversation had then stalled, and ended.

Finally, Bessy broke the long silence, perking up as the carriage made its way around a bend, the manor house now in clear sight.

"There," she said. "Down House."

Field and Barnum raised themselves up to peer over the heads of the horses, trying to get a glimpse of the house, a large three-level manor with an ivy-covered bay at the front that stretched all the way to the roof. Smoke rose from two of its three chimneys, and a luxurious jet-black carriage sat in front, its driver and footman talking quietly beside it, the smoke from pipes drifting around them.

"We are in luck," said Field. "Unless I miss my guess, they are very much at home, for someone has newly arrived or is about to leave, and a meal is being prepared."

"I would agree," said Barnum. "And I grow giddy with anticipation. I have no doubt now that we shall find our Lily once more."

"Indeed, sir. I share that fine sentiment. It has been a long search: that is a fact. I dare say, I hope we are not disappointed."

"Look!" shouted Williams, pointing toward the house. "Over there!"

Field held a hand to his brow to block the afternoon sun. Six men in black, or more, were racing at the house from all directions. Swords and spears gleamed in the sunlight.

"Quickly now!" shouted Field.

Williams cracked the whip and the horses hurtled forward.

79

Down House, Downe, 4:00 P.M., Monday, April 6, 1857.

I can control my transformations, yes. But when I am angered to transform, it is always the same. One second I am a woman, the next, a singular beast, with but one goal: to kill. Everything else — friendships, right and wrong, even love — gives way to a blood lust I cannot fully describe and not fully control. It is as if a curtain rises on a play with but two characters — the killer and the killed — and I alone write the script for its bloody end. If you see me then, do not step upon that stage, for I am nothing less than a berserker, and you are nothing more to me than an obstacle of flesh and sinew to be torn apart. And tear I will.

— Lily, Interview with the Dragon (excerpt)

After several inquiries in Downe, Biniam Sahle and his men found themselves in a copse of trees overlooking the garden at Down House. He had begun to motion his men forward, directing them to spread out, to give them the best chance of surrounding the house and preventing escape. Then he saw an albino woman pacing in the garden. He could not be sure at this distance, but she looked much like the woman he had chased through the streets of London many years ago, although much older.

"Adunga," he whispered, grabbing the man by the arm. "The woman there, in the garden, do you see her."

Adunga nodded silently.

"I would have her head."

Adunga smiled and drew his sword. "It is yours."

Biniam watched him go, running in a crouch, picking up speed, hurtling himself toward the woman, sword held high.

What a day this shall be, Biniam thought.

• • •

Enku continued pacing, occasionally glancing back at the open window to the drawing room, where she could see Lily in all her finery.

This is not right, she thought. *This will not happen. This cannot happen.*

She had tried again and again to make Lily see the light, her one true self, but Lily had resisted. The incredible force she had once held in her arms was being transformed into just another English woman, obedient and useless.

Enku spat in the direction of the house. Perhaps it will go wrong. Perhaps she will make some unforgivable mistake. A wrong choice of fork or spoon.

Enku shook her head. *No, she has been well schooled and loves to get things right. We are doomed.*

A sound startled her. She turned to see a tall man dressed all in black rushing toward her, his sword held high, beginning his swing.

She turned back to the house and screamed, "Lily!"

• • •

Darwin froze for a brief moment, watching as the sword swept through Enku's neck, her head lifting into the air in a spray of blood. He glanced quickly around the room. Lily was gone, her dress on the floor, clearly ripped away. Emma was across the room, bending over the baronet, who had apparently swooned.

"Stay here," he shouted at Emma, who nodded silently, completely terrified.

Darwin rushed from the room for his study, where he kept his birding gun, always loaded but locked away in a tall cabinet. He fumbled with the lock, but finally threw back the doors, grabbed the gun, and raced outside. He would have only one shot, so he had to make it count.

By the time he reached the garden, Lily had already dispatched three of the assailants, their twisted, disemboweled bodies slumped upon the ground. She held a fourth by the neck in her jaws, and was shaking him violently, his head finally separating from his body. She spit out the head and flew at a fifth man, grabbing him by the leg and lifting him into the air, the man screaming in terror and jabbing at her with a short dagger, to no effect.

Darwin looked for other assailants, quickly spotting two more men in black, one old, Enku's head in his grasp, and a younger, taller man, who was aiming an arrow at Lily. Darwin raised his gun, took a deep breath, and fired. The young man dropped, but not before loosing his arrow, which just missed Lily.

Lily ripped her victim apart midair and roared down at Darwin, who stumbled backwards. *Is she after me?* A chill ran up his spine as she launched herself at him. *The gun. She thinks I am a threat.*

He dropped the gun and ran toward the house, where to his horror, he could see his children and Miss Thorley rushing from the house, apparently attracted to the garden by the gunfire.

"No," Darwin shouted at them, "back in the house, now!"

He could hear the buffeting of her wings as she neared him, and then she was gone, distracted by other gunshots. Two men were rushing through the garden, firing at the last assailant, who was running away with Enku's head. Lily ignored the two men and roared.

•   •   •

Biniam had miscalculated, badly. He had trained his men well, but Lily had changed. She was bigger, stronger, faster. They were no match for her.

He heard her roar behind him and tried his best to run faster, but age had caught him long ago, and now he was being lifted into the air, talons digging into him.

He thought to scream, but it was only a thought lost in a rapidly closing darkness.

•   •   •

She ripped him in half, letting half of him fall to the ground with Enku's head, and throwing the other half across the field, where it tumbled into a thicket. She hovered in the air, looking back to assess additional threats, but there were none.

The two men had lowered their pistols and were making no moves to reload. They were just standing there, looking up at her, mouths agape. She recognized Barnum right away and thought to land near him, but then she caught sight of Darwin and Emma emerging from the house, and her heart sank.

Darwin had his arms spread wide, motioning for her to calm herself, but Emma was glaring up at her, fuming, her arms held close to her sides, fists clenched. Lily could see her future at

Down House condensed into that one look. She was no longer welcome here. It was time to move on, for good or ill.

She landed, picked up Enku's head, cradling it gently in her arms, and lifted back into the air.

Darwin was running toward her, shouting her name, but Lily turned away from him, flapped her wings with great force, and disappeared into the clouds.

80

Down House, Downe, 4:30 P.M., Monday, April 6, 1857.

Detective Chief Inspector Field had taken control of the situation, sending Barnum and the Darwins back inside as he and Detective Constable Williams assessed the carnage.

"Williams, take the carriage and your Bessy back to Downe. Find the constable. I think his name is Smythe or Wythe or some such."

"Yes, sir."

"Tell him what has transpired here, and have him make the necessary arrangements. We shall need, what, eight caskets?"

"Yes, that is my count as well."

"Right, so then take Bessy home and return here. I want to be back at Whitehall before dark, if possible."

Williams nodded and trotted toward the carriage. Field watched him go, then made his way through the garden and into the house, following the sounds of muffled voices in the drawing room.

Darwin saw him first and came over to shake his hand.

"Thank you for coming. I think you saved the day."

Field smiled, clearly pleased. "We stand to serve, sir, but I would not discount your own part in this unfortunate drama. That was quite a shot."

Darwin offered a weak smile. He was quite exhausted. "I have been hunting since I was a boy. A man is an easy target compared to a bird on the wing."

"I assume so." Field could tell the man was upset. "Tell me, do you think she will return?"

Darwin frowned. "I do not know. I hope so, but I fear I am wrong."

Field glanced over Darwin's shoulder. Emma was sitting in a chair against the wall, staring into space, clearly shaken to her core. "Indeed." He pointed at Emma. "I think you best attend her. She seems much distraught, as is only natural. It must have been quite a fright for her, and for the children. Are they all right?"

"Yes, a fright to be sure. And yes, the children are fine. Our Miss Thorley has them well in hand and has calmed them."

"Good, good," said Field. "Now, if you do not mind, I must have a word with Mr. Barnum."

"Of course. I must see to Emma."

Darwin walked across the room and laid a hand on Emma's shoulder, which she shrugged off, giving him an angry look, one that Field recognized immediately, given his experience with the indomitable Mrs. Field. He turned away and pulled up a chair next to Barnum, who was wiping his forehead, still in awe of what he had just witnessed.

Field cleared his throat. "May I assume there shall be no reward?"

Barnum glanced at him as if he were coming out of a daze. "What? Oh, yes, the reward. That is something I shall have to reconsider."

"But if I find her again, surely . . ." Field's voice trailed off.

Barnum gathered himself, adjusting his cravat and smoothing his hair. "There can be no reward for the older woman, this Enku woman. What a *horrible* death."

"No, of course not."

"But as for the other woman, my angel, I have no idea how you will capture her, even if you should find her again."

Field knew he was probably right, but a reward was a reward, and Mrs. Field had her needs. "Leave that to me."

Barnum nodded. "Very well, I shall let the reward stand."

"Excellent, sir, excellent."

The sound of a cane tapping hard on the floor drew everyone's attention to the small, frail man sitting in the corner, looking back at them with a puzzled look on his face.

"I say," said the baronet, "will there be dinner or not?"

81

Twenty-five years later. Down House, Downe, 3:15 P.M., Wednesday, April 19, 1882.

Emma sat alone in her husband's study, looking at all the things that defined him, trying to make sense of it all. He was failing, that was clear. The heart pain had come again in the night, and he had roused her. "I have got the pain," he had said, "and I shall feel better, or bear it better, if you are awake."

She had attended him, but minutes later he had had another attack and seemed to lose consciousness. She had sat with him during the night, the hands on the clock never seeming to move. When he had finally awakened, he had insisted that at age seventy-three he would not see another sunrise. "I am not the least afraid of death," he had said.

Emma had not known what to say to him. Words would not come, so she had sat quietly beside him, holding his hand. When he had dozed off, she had sent one of the servants to fetch Etty, who had arrived in short order, Etty giving him his salts and rubbing him, and giving him a little whisky. "If I could but die," he had pleaded again and again.

And then, as the clock in the study struck one, there was a firm knocking on the front door. Emma rose from her chair and walked down the long hall to the door. When she opened it, her eyes went wide. "You," was all she could say.

"May I come in?" said Lily.

Emma hesitated. Although twenty-five years had passed, her anger at Lily had not subsided in the least. And now here she was, looking not a day older than the last time Emma had seen her on that bloody day. Emma, at seventy-four, had grown old and gray, but Lily was still young and strikingly beautiful, even in this abomination of dress—*dressed like a man!*—from top hat to long coat, to frock coat, to trousers and boots.

Emma calmed herself. She knew Charles would want to see her, and perhaps seeing her might rally him. "Come, he is longing to die."

Emma led him to his bed, where Etty sat tending him. When she caught sight of Lily, her mouth dropped open. She had been just fourteen when Lily had left, and now she was thirty-nine, long past her prime.

"Lily, is that you?"

Emma didn't give Lily time for reply, grabbing Etty's hand and moving her toward the door. "Come, we shall make tea."

When they reached the door, Emma turned back toward Lily. "He is very weak. Do not be long."

Lily nodded and turned her attention to Charles, rubbing his hand and whispering his name until he awoke. He smiled up at her. "Oh, Lily, my Lily."

"It is good to see you again," she said.

He attempted a chuckle but ended with a cough that wracked him.

"There, there, rest easy."

"The pain will not let me rest, but seeing you is indeed a balm." He glanced at her clothes and attempted a laugh. "I see you have still not warmed to dresses."

"Just another disguise, but I do wear dresses from time to time, as is sometimes required of the Countess de Beuzeville."

"Countess?"

Lily giggled. "Yes, I followed Emma's plan, in France."

Charles smiled weakly. "I was so worried about you."

"I am sorry I did not return sooner."

"No, you had to make your own way in the world, and I see now that the Chinaman was telling the truth. You have not aged a day."

"I traveled some, even went to Tierra del Fuego to find my father. The cave was there, just as you had said, but I found only my father's bones."

Charles frowned. "He said he could be killed, but that sickness would never take him."

"It was so. The marks were clear. He had been hacked to death, by several men if I am not mistaken."

"I am sorry." He coughed again, eyes tearing.

"No," she said, dabbing at Darwin's eyes with a handkerchief. "I did not know him, but I do know now that the story you told me, which you and I both thought fantastical, must be true."

Charles shook his head weakly. "Perhaps, and you are certainly plain evidence of that, but *dragons?* Imagine a world with dragons." He coughed hard.

Lily rubbed his hand. "Easy now. I came tonight not knowing of your illness, and I am sorry for it. I had hoped to discuss dragons with you — and my brother."

Charles patted her hand with a feeble quivering motion. "I have told you *all* I remembered and even that has near flown from my head. If I had my journal, you would know all, but it was lost the same day you cracked from your egg." Charles rose up in bed and clutched at his chest. "Oh, God, the pain."

Lily eased him back to his pillow and stroked his forehead. "I have never thanked you for saving me."

He attempted to raise his hand, but dropped it back to the bed, his breath growing stertorous, the rattle of death growing near. "Dragons," he whispered, and then he was gone.

EPILOGUE

British Geological Survey, Nottingham, England, October 14, Present Day.

Bruce Cargo had had just about enough, his hands shaking with anger as his boss, Dr. Shepherd, not so affectionately known as "Old Nozzle," turned and walked away.

Clean up the gloomy corner, he had said. Today.

Bruce's first thought was to quietly pack his things and leave a brief note of resignation for the bastard. *Fuck that, I'm a scientist, not an intern.*

But then he had had second thoughts, the most compelling being the desire to keep his job. If he botched this opportunity, he'd probably have to go back to the States, and he didn't want that. And there was Luna to consider. She would not think kindly if he blew this, perhaps his last chance to grab a foothold on any semblance of a career, at least in England.

So he had calmed himself and set about the task, yanking off his tie, rolling up his sleeves, and arming himself with a flashlight, a makeshift dust cloth, and a bottle of water from the machine.

At five foot ten, he was not a big man, but he was athletic, with broad shoulders, well-defined muscles, and the obligatory six-pack abs of a devoted gym rat. Not many people would have called him handsome, but there was something about him that attracted women, who invariably called him sexy, noting his square jaw, long sandy hair, and ice blue eyes. Rugged good looks, they would say, an aura about him.

The first two hours had been exactly what he had expected: a cloud of dust, the smell of mildew and aging samples and slides, and myriad boxes and other containers to sort through and rearrange into like categories, butterflies here, small mammal bones there, and so on.

And then he had happened upon a small barrel, sealed top and bottom to protect the specimens inside from a sea voyage, but broken open nonetheless, and in a strange way. At first he thought that someone had hit the side of the barrel hard with an ax, but it was soon apparent that the force had come from inside the barrel, not outside, the wood bursting outward. Stranger still, there were no splinters or wood chips on the floor around the barrel, indicating that perhaps the barrel had been moved to the gloomy corner after whatever burst out had burst out.

He peered into the opening in the barrel and pulled out fragments of a modest-sized egg encrusted with what looked like long-dead barnacles, perhaps an ostrich egg, although the color seemed wrong, and a small package wrapped in sail cloth and tightly bound in hemp twine.

The writing on the package sent a shock through him. *C. Darwin, Esq. Do not open.*

ABOUT THE AUTHOR

Len Boswell is the author of eleven books, including award-winning mysteries, fantasies, and memoirs. He lives in the mountains of West Virginia with his wife, Ruth, and their two dogs, Shadow and Cinder.

NOTE FROM THE AUTHOR

Word-of-mouth is crucial for any author to succeed. If you enjoyed *Barnum's Angel*, please leave a review online—anywhere you are able. Even if it's just a sentence or two. It would make all the difference and would be very much appreciated.

Thanks!
Len Boswell

We hope you enjoyed reading this title from:

BLACK ROSE
writing™

www.blackrosewriting.com

Subscribe to our mailing list – *The Rosevine* – and receive **FREE** books, daily
deals, and stay current with news about upcoming
releases and our hottest authors.
Scan the QR code below to sign up.

Already a subscriber? Please accept a sincere thank you for being a fan of
Black Rose Writing authors.

View other Black Rose Writing titles at
www.blackrosewriting.com/books and use promo code
PRINT to receive a **20% discount** when purchasing.